# After the Fall

Berneice Rosenbaum

# Contents

# Chapter 1

When the final bell of the day rang, I was the first one up and out of my seat, much to the amusement of my classmates. I hurried out into the hall and made my way to my locker, dodging the other students as I went.

When I reached my locker, I shoved my books onto the shelf and then grabbed my bag. As I went to turn around, an arm slid around my waist and I looked up to see my boyfriend, Adam, smiling down at me. "Hey."

I smiled up at him as we headed down the hallway together. "Hey yourself. How was your afternoon?"

He rolled his eyes. "Boring as hell. I wish we had classes together after lunch. I like my mornings a lot better because you're with me."

I chuckled at him. "Such a charmer," I said teasingly. "You're just hoping to get lucky when I get back from the show this weekend."

He grinned widely. "Can't blame a guy for trying."

I laughed. "I suppose not." We had reached the door and he opened it, standing back so I could exit first. "I wish you could come with me this weekend," I said as I stepped outside.

"Me too, baby. But we have the big game tomorrow. I might be able to make it out on Sunday."

I shook my head. "No, I don't want you to have to drive all the way out there for one day. And I'll be too busy on Sunday to give you the attention you deserve."

Adam brushed a lock of my hair away from my face. "Any attention is better than none at all."

I giggled. "God, that was so cheesy!"

He grinned cockily. "Yeah, but you love it when I'm cheesy." He led me into the parking lot and stopped, turning me so he could kiss me. "I'm going to miss you this weekend. Who else will wear my number for me?"

"Oh, I'm sure you could find a lot of girls to wear it for you."

He rubbed his nose against mine. "In their dreams. You're the only one I want to be with."

"It's a good thing I know that, or I might have to be jealous." I pulled his face down to mine and kissed him again.

"Oi! How many times do I have to tell you that I don't like seeing PDA's?"

I broke the kiss and turned to glare at my twin brother Luke, who was leaning against his car. "Mind your own business!" I kissed Adam once more and hugged him. "I'll be home really late on Sunday, but I'll let you know how the weekend is going, okay?"

He sighed and held me tighter to him. "Okay. I love you."

"I love you too. Kick some butt at the game tomorrow, okay?"

"I'll try. Have fun at the show and be careful."

"I will. See you on Monday." We exchanged one last kiss before I hurried over to where Luke was standing, pretending to gag. "Oh, grow up."

He slung his arm around my shoulder and ruffled my hair like he always did. "Dana, you know I care about you. But that was seriously gross."

I laughed and shoved his arm off of me. "Come on little brother, we need to get home and get the horses loaded."

"Ten minutes older than me and you never let me live it down," he grumbled as he went to his side of the car.

I slid into the passenger seat as he got into the driver's seat. We drove the ten minutes to our house, talking about the upcoming show. It was the first major one of the season and we were both excited about it.

We pulled into our driveway and Luke parked by the house. We hurried inside and changed, then grabbed the bags we had packed already and brought them back out to his car. He threw them into the back seat before we walked down to the stable, where chaos currently reigned.

The two trucks and trailers were already hooked up and waiting, so I knew we'd be ready to load up soon. I waved to my best friend Cindy as she hurried by, her arms full of tack. She grinned at me before disappearing into the tack room of one of the trailers.

I walked into the barn and found my mom. "Hey mom, we're home!"

She turned and smiled in relief. "Good. Go grab your horses; we're ready to load them up."

I nodded and scurried down to where my bay mare was waiting for me. I grabbed her lead rope and opened the stall door. "Hey Destiny. Ready for our big weekend?" I clipped the lead rope onto her halter and led her into the aisle where I attached her to the crossties and went to my tack box, pulling out her shipping boots. I quickly put them on and unclipped the ties, leading her into the yard.

Luke had his feisty gray gelding, Justice, out there already. He loaded him onto the trailer quickly and once he was out of the way, I put Destiny on. I made sure she had hay for the trip, and then gave her a quick pat before exiting the trailer. Cindy loaded her black gelding, Max, after me and then we closed up the trailer doors.

I made my way to the tack room to make sure I hadn't forgotten anything. Satisfied that I had everything I needed, I went back into the yard. My dad was just loading his big chestnut mare, Savannah, onto the second trailer. My mom's gelding, Duke, was loaded already and so was the one other horse that was going, Star. He belonged to another student, Sarah, who was meeting us at the show. I was good friends with her as well.

Once the horses were loaded and we had triple checked that we had everything, my parents climbed into one of the trucks. I waved as they slowly made their way down the tree-lined driveway.

One of our grooms got into the other truck and followed my parents. Cindy got into her car and I followed my brother back to his car. We climbed in and took off, following behind Cindy.

It was a two- hour drive to the show grounds, and I was bouncing in my seat the whole way. I was so excited for the first show of the year. We arrived at the grounds and there was a flurry of activity as we got the horses unloaded and settled into their temporary stalls. I made sure Destiny was comfortable and then helped unload all the tack.

It was starting to get dark by the time we were finally done. We were all tired, so we went out for a quick dinner and then retired to the motel we were staying in. Our groom, Rusty, was staying in the tack stall at the grounds, just to be safe.

Cindy, Sarah and I were sharing a room. I claimed one of the beds immediately and Sarah quickly jumped onto the other one. Cindy scowled as she grudgingly went over to the cot and plopped down. "So not fair."

I laughed at her. "You snooze, you lose." I looked at my watch. "I'm going to call Adam quickly and let him know we're settled."

After I had talked to him, I changed into my pajamas. I yawned hugely and climbed under the covers. Cindy and Sarah did the same and I flicked off the lights. "Good night."

They murmured back to me and then I was out like a light.

The next day went by quickly. I had three classes that I was entered in, and I placed third, fourth and seventh. I was very pleased, as this was my first show season with Destiny. Luke ended up winning his classes with Justice, and of course he had to gloat about it.

I called Adam after dinner and told him about my day. "I was a little mad at myself in the last class. I set Destiny up completely wrong for the combination, which is why I took two of the elements down."

"You're still getting to know the horse, Dana. Don't beat yourself up about it." His voice became muffled as he spoke to someone. He came back on the line. "Sorry baby, I have to go. I hope you have a good day tomorrow. I love you."

"Love you too. And I'm glad you won your game. Talk to you tomorrow."

When I woke up the next morning, I had a feeling that something was wrong, but I couldn't place it, so I ignored it and went about my day. Destiny and I had a better day, even managing to win one of our classes, which I was ecstatic about. Luke and Justice had a bit of an off day, but they still managed to be Champion in their division.

After the horses were all loaded up again, we all piled into our respective vehicles and headed home. Halfway there, Luke swore under his breath. "I need to stop for gas."

"Okay, that'll give me a chance to grab a snack. I'm starving." We pulled up to the next gas station that we came to. I went in to grab something to eat for both of us as he filled the gas tank.

As we pulled back out onto the highway, I sent Adam a text, saying we were halfway home and that I couldn't wait to see him tomorrow. He sent one back saying the same and that he loved me.

It was almost completely dark and we were about twenty minutes from home. I turned to tell Luke something and his eyes suddenly went wide as saucers. "Shit!"

That was the last thing I heard before my world came crashing down around me.

# Chapter 2

Hollow.

That was the first feeling I became aware of. The first was severe pain in my left leg. I struggled to open my eyes, but I couldn't focus enough to manage it. I groaned quietly and then became aware of someone squeezing my hand. Using that as a focal point, I finally managed to pry one of my eyelids open slowly.

All I could see was white. I forced my other eye open and I realized that it was a white ceiling. I knew this wasn't my room, but I couldn't concentrate long enough to try and figure out where I was. With a sigh, I closed my eyes once more.

When I woke up the next time, my mind felt clearer, but I still felt hollow. My eyes opened with little effort this time and I was able to see that I was in a hospital room. I had an IV in my left hand and there were machines all around me.

Movement to my right side had me slowly turning my head in that direction. I saw my parents, Cindy and Adam all standing beside my bed, with a mixture of relief and concern on all their faces.

I opened my mouth to say something and that's when I realized there was a tube in my throat. I panicked and tried to rip it out, but my dad and Adam quickly restrained me as a doctor walked in.

"Hello Dana, I'm Dr. Green. I know you're probably confused right now, but don't try and talk until we remove the tube from your throat."

I nodded and waited while a nurse came in. They removed the tube from my throat and adjusted my bed so that I was sitting up more. Cindy and my mother moved closer so that they were standing next to Adam and my dad. I looked at my parents. "What..." That's all I got out before I started coughing again.

My dad quickly poured a glass of water and handed it to me. I sipped it gratefully. "What happened?" I managed to croak out.

"There was an accident on the way back from the show. Do you remember?"

The memories flooded back and I squeezed my eyes shut tightly. I remembered the sounds of crashing metal, the blinding light as a vehicle hit us head on. I remembered the look in Luke's eyes as he met my gaze a split second before we were hit. My eyes flew open and I looked at my dad. "Luke?"

The grief on his face told me everything before he spoke. "He didn't make it."

My eyes rolled back into my head and I fainted before he even finished speaking.

"Dana, it's time for you to wake up now. Open your eyes sweetie."

The voice was slightly desperate, so I fought to the surface of the fog that had enveloped me. I opened my eyes to see my dad standing over me. As soon as I saw him, I remembered that Luke was gone and tears flooded my eyes. My dad tried to hug me, but I pushed him away, ignoring the hurt look on his face.

I fought to regain control of myself and when I could speak again, I looked at my mom. "When's the funeral?"

"It was three weeks ago, sweetheart."

I frowned in confusion. "Huh?"

"You've been in a coma for the past month."

My eyes widened. "A month?" I whispered. How could I have lost a month of my life? Then I thought about the fact that Luke had lost the rest of his life and I decided I didn't care how long I'd been unconscious for. In fact, I wished I'd never woken up so that I'd be with my brother.

Dr. Green came back into my hospital room. "Good, you're awake again. We have a lot to discuss."

I looked at the people who cared so much about me, but I couldn't face them properly right now. "Can you get them to leave for a bit?" I asked the doctor quietly.

If he was surprised, he didn't show it as he turned to the four other people in the room. "If you could all just wait outside for a bit that would be great. I want to talk to Dana alone for a few minutes."

They reluctantly left the room and I let out a sigh of relief. "Thank you."

"I understand that this can't be easy for you. Sometimes the ones that care about you the most will suffocate you without meaning to." He set down the chart he had been holding. "Now, can you tell me how you feel?"

"Empty."

I saw something flicker in his eyes, but he just nodded. "Okay, and what about physically?"

I took a minute to consider his words. "Sore everywhere, but my left leg is by far the worst," I replied.

"But you can feel that leg?"

I looked at him in confusion. "Yeah, why wouldn't I be able to?"

He sighed and sat down in the chair beside the bed. "Your lower left leg was completely crushed in the accident. At first we thought we were going to have to amputate, but we had a specialist here who wanted to try and save your leg. Miraculously, he was able to do so, but we weren't sure how much sensation would be left, even after all the surgeries."

It took me a moment to absorb his words. "Does that mean I won't be able to walk again?"

"Normally I would say that you wouldn't be able to, but the fact that you can feel your leg means that you might retain the ability to move it. If that's the case, then with a lot of physical therapy you could be able to walk again."

I closed my eyes and didn't say anything else. I didn't care if I never walked again. My twin, the person who I had shared my entire life with, the person who was my other half, was now gone. And apparently my ability to care had left with him. Like I had told the doctor earlier, I was empty.

I heard the doctor leave and then heard the whispers as my parents, Cindy and Adam came back in. I kept my eyes closed and pretended to sleep so they wouldn't try and talk to me. And then I eventually did go back to sleep, and I welcomed the nothingness that awaited me.

I stayed in the hospital for the next three weeks. During that time, Cindy and Adam continued to visit me along with my parents. I stopped talking unless absolutely necessary and I knew that it worried everyone, but I just couldn't bring myself to care.

One day I told Cindy and Adam to stop visiting me. Adam protested violently, but I refused to speak to him anymore. Eventually he gave up and stopped coming.

Cindy, on the other hand, acted as if I'd never said anything. She continued to visit me every single day. She would come in the mornings and she always brought a book with her. She would sit beside my bed for hours and read silently. She never pressed me into conversation, so I didn't bother telling her to leave me alone again.

My parents tried really hard to find ways to cheer me up, but nothing helped. Even hearing about the horses gained no reaction from me. They tried having a psychiatrist talk to me, but since I refused to speak to him, it didn't work that well.

I eventually learned that it had been a drunk driver that had hit Luke's car. Luke had been killed instantly, which gave me a small measure of comfort. At least he hadn't suffered. The driver of the other vehicle had died as well, and I was morbidly pleased about that fact.

I suffered from nightmares that were so bad that the doctors started giving me sedatives at night so that I could sleep peacefully. I was told that when I went home I would have a prescription of strong sleeping pills to continue to help me until the nightmares lessened.

On my last night in the hospital I laid awake, waiting for the sedative to take effect. I thought over all that had happened in the last three weeks. I knew my parents were incredibly worried about me, and for the first time I actually felt a twinge of guilt. But it was gone as quickly as it had come.

No one understood that I wasn't like this intentionally. I didn't want to hurt the people who loved me, but I couldn't help it. There was just nothing left inside me. Luke and I had never been apart for more than two nights before, and now he was gone for good. The connection we'd always had had disappeared, and it would never come back.

How could I explain that to anyone who didn't understand? I couldn't, so I didn't even try. Silence became my savior. If I didn't talk, they couldn't expect me to answer their questions. If I didn't talk, I didn't have to acknowledge the pain out loud. And if I didn't talk, then no one would ever know that I wished I'd died with my brother.

# Chapter 3

F ive months later

I stared out the window at the rainy weather, thinking that it suited my mood perfectly. Today was to be my first day back to school since the accident. I had missed the first month and a half of classes, but my parents had hired a tutor so that I was caught up on all my work. Now they were forcing me to leave the haven I'd created in the house.

For the past five months, I'd enclosed myself in my new room, which was on the main floor of the house now, since I couldn't manage the stairs. Despite my many protests, I'd been forced into physical therapy and I could now get around with crutches. Aside from those sessions, I only left my room when I was hungry. I had a bathroom attached to my room, so I didn't even need to leave for that.

With a sigh, I struggled to my feet and made my way into the bathroom. I looked at myself in the mirror and I was slightly startled at my own appearance. My dark brown hair was longer than it had ever been, since I hadn't gotten it cut since before the accident. My face was pale from lack of sunlight and it was gaunt as well, as I'd lost a bit of weight. My hazel eyes were blank, where before they had always been lively and full of expression.

With a shake of my head, I turned away from my reflection and got into the shower. When I was done, I got dressed in jeans and a t-shirt, then put one of Luke's hoodies on over top. I hadn't been able to bring myself to go into his room, but my dad had brought me some of his stuff when I asked. It was one of the few times I had voluntarily spoken to anyone, so I knew he wouldn't deny my request.

After I had brushed my hair, I went into the kitchen where my dad was waiting for me. He looked up as I came in. "Ready?"

I shrugged and took an apple to eat on the way, and then grabbed my bag and followed him out the door. He took my crutches from me and put them in the backseat once I was settled in the front passenger seat.

He didn't try to talk to me as we drove to the school. My parents had learned that if I wanted to talk, I would. They no longer tried to push me into conversation, which I was grateful for.

When we pulled up at the school, my dad parked the car and got my crutches for me. Once he was sure I had my bag settled on my back and my crutches securely under my arms, he stepped back. "Have a good day. Cindy will drive you home after."

I nodded and slowly made my way into the school. Someone was kind enough to hold the door open for me and I murmured my thanks to them. I already knew where my locker was, but I didn't need to do anything there yet so I just made my way to my first class.

I reached the classroom and went in, moving to the back of the room and sitting in a seat in the corner after taking my bag off my back and setting my crutches against the wall. I stuffed my hands into the front pocket of Luke's sweater and leaned back, closing my eyes. I heard someone come into the room, but I kept my eyes closed. I knew it was Cindy, because I could smell her perfume. She didn't say anything; she just sat in the seat beside me.

I could hear other students entering the room and I swear I could feel their gazes burning into me. I kept my eyes closed until the bell rang; then I finally opened them and scanned the room. It was full of people I knew and a few of them had visited me in the hospital.

I spotted Adam sitting near the front. He turned to look at me and I could see that he wanted to come up to me. But I turned away before he could get the chance to. My eyes rested on the only person I didn't recognize at all.

I could tell he was tall, even though he was slouching a little in his chair. He had short, dark blonde hair and brilliant green eyes and I wondered briefly who he was. He hadn't been here last year, so I knew he must have only started here at the beginning of the year.

The teacher entered the room, drawing my attention away from the new guy. This was a history class and I had always liked the subject. The teacher, Mr. Ross, had been my favorite at one time, but now I just didn't care.

Mr. Ross gazed across the room and his eyes landed on me. I couldn't read the expression in his eyes, but I was grateful that he didn't give me any words of sympathy. All he said was "Welcome back."

This seemed to give everyone permission to turn and stare at me. I flipped the hood up over my head, effectively shielding my face from the curious stares.

Mr. Ross clapped his hands together. "Okay class, let's get right to the projects. Split off into your pairs and get started." He glanced at me again. "Dana, I'm going to put you with Chase, as he's the only one without a partner." He gestured to the new guy.

I turned to look at him and caught Cindy's gaze. She gave me an apologetic look as she got up and moved to sit with Adam. I raised an eyebrow. She hadn't told me that she was partnered with him, but I understood why she hadn't. She had told me that Adam constantly asked about me, and she knew I didn't want to really hear about him.

My attention was drawn to my side as Cindy's now empty chair was pulled back. Chase sat down in it and met my gaze for the first time. I felt a jolt of something race through me as our eyes connected. It took me a moment to place the feeling. Recognition. I could see in his eyes the same demons that tormented me daily.

He must have realized it too, because his expression changed slightly, becoming a little bit softer. Not with sympathy, but with understanding. Without a word, he handed me a small stack of papers, which I proceeded to read.

Neither of us uttered a single word during the whole class. He just sat there as I got caught up. When the bell rang, I handed him his papers back and stood up. I left the room in silence and Cindy was waiting for me. Her eyes were full of apologies and I frowned, not sure what was going on. Then I felt a hand on my shoulder and I turned around to see Adam standing there. I shrugged his hand off of me and started to move away from him.

"Dana, wait. Please talk to me," he pleaded.

I shook my head. "I can't," I whispered and then hobbled away.

The rest of the day passed slowly. At lunch, Cindy and Sarah both sat with me, talking amongst themselves. I knew people were still staring at me and not all of them were sympathetic. I ignored all of them and picked at my food.

I had math third period and English for fourth. I had math with Cindy, and Sarah was in my second period Geography class, but neither of them were in my English class.

When fourth period rolled around, I entered the room and again went to a seat in the back corner. When someone sat down beside me, I looked up. Chase glanced at me as he set his binder on the desk, but he didn't say anything. I shrugged and decided it wasn't a big deal if he wanted to sit next to me.

The whole class passed and again we didn't talk, just like in history class. I looked at him a few times but he kept his gaze forward. The bell rang and he stood up quickly. I expected him to leave right away, but he surprised me by taking my bag and holding it while I got to my feet. Then he handed it to me and walked away. I stared after him in bewilderment, then shook my head and left the room as well.

Cindy was waiting for me in the parking lot. My gaze flickered to where Luke had always parked and my heart clenched when I saw a different vehicle sitting there. I walked to Cindy's car and got into the passenger seat. She started the car and pulled out of the parking lot.

She stayed silent for a few minutes before finally speaking. "How was it?"

I shrugged. "Okay."

She nodded and didn't say anything else. When we got to my place, she dropped me off at the house and then continued on down to the stables.

The next day in history class, I got there early again and went to the same seat. I felt someone sit next to me and assumed it was Cindy. But I couldn't smell her perfume so I looked over. Chase was sitting next to me, and I gave him a questioning look, but he didn't say anything so I turned back to gaze at the front of the room.

Cindy came in and looked startled to see Chase sitting next to me. She looked at me and I shrugged, so she took the seat in front of me.

The class started and we broke into pairs again. I had done some research of my own last night, so I handed it to Chase. He passed me some new papers and we spent the class in reading each other's work and taking notes. When the bell rang I got up to leave and I could sense him following behind me.

I walked through the door and almost ran into Adam, who was waiting for me again. He opened his mouth to say something, but then his gaze flickered to something behind me. His jaw snapped shut and he paled a tiny bit.

I turned to see what had caused his reaction and I saw Chase standing right behind me and the look he was giving Adam sent shivers down my spine. I had never seen anyone look quite that scary before.

Adam spun on his heel and walked off down the hall. I glanced back at Chase once more and I swear I saw the beginning of a smirk on his face. But he wiped it off quickly as he looked down at me. I wanted to ask why he had done that, but I decided not to. Instead I just turned and went to the cafeteria.

I sat down across from Sarah and Cindy. They were chatting about something when they both suddenly stopped and froze. Chase took the seat next to me and I furrowed my brow. Why the hell had he decided to sit next to me? And what had possessed him to give Adam that look? None of this made any sense to me, but I couldn't bring myself to ask him why he kept sitting neat me. I knew if he wanted to tell me then he would. We ate our meals quietly and Cindy and Sarah slowly started talking again, although they kept glancing between me and Chase.

The rest of the afternoon was uneventful. Chase sat next to me in English again and he helped me with my bag once more before walking out of the room.

After school, Cindy told me what she knew about him, though I hadn't asked. "It's weird how Chase seems to like you. No one knows much about him. He lives with a foster family and he came to our school at the beginning of the year. He doesn't talk to anyone; and I mean that literally. He actually refuses to speak. Everyone knows he can talk, he just chooses not to. He got into a few fights at the beginning of the year but he beat the crap out of anyone who tried to go after him, so everyone leaves him alone now."

I suddenly felt a strange kinship with Chase, knowing that he didn't like talking either. I wondered what his story was, but I knew I would never ask him. A person's pain belonged to them, and if he didn't want to share it with anyone, then I certainly wasn't going to push him.

# Chapter 4

The rest of the week passed by in the same way. Chase sat next to me in history and we worked on our project without speaking, then he joined me at lunch and sat next to me again in English. He always helped me with my bag at the end of each class, and he even started carrying it to my locker for me at the end of the day. I knew everyone was as confused as I was about why he seemed drawn to me, especially since we hadn't spoken a single word to each other.

The weekend went by the same as it usually did. Cindy came to hang out with me for a bit on Saturday, but that was the most exciting thing that happened.

Monday morning rolled around and I got ready for school. I had started wearing Luke's hoodies every day; they made me feel closer to him in a way. When I got to school I headed straight for my class without stopping at my locker first. I sat down and a few minutes later, Chase sat beside me. I glanced over and I was a little startled when his lips turned up in a brief smile. My lips tried to tug up in response, but the smile didn't really form before it was gone again.

Mr. Ross and the rest of the class slowly filed in and then the bell rang. Mr. Ross spoke up. "Okay, you should be making headway on the research aspect of the project by now, so today you can work on presentation. I'll put some of you in the hall and some of you can go to the library."

My eyes widened at his words. We were supposed to do a presentation? How the hell was that supposed to work when neither Chase nor I liked talking? Luckily, Mr. Ross came up to us after he had spread everyone else out. "You two don't have to do a presentation. I'll just mark you on your research and the paper you'll write up."

Relief flooded me, and then Chase shocked me by actually speaking. "Thanks," he said in a voice so quiet that no one other than the teacher and myself would have heard him. His voice was deep and rough and the sound of it sent a shiver down my spine.

If Mr. Ross was surprised, he didn't show it. "You're welcome," he replied and then walked off to help someone else.

Chase and I worked on our project quietly once more and then went our separate ways afterwards, meeting up once again in the cafeteria. Sarah and Cindy were absent as they were on the yearbook committee and they had a meeting.

I opened my container of cookies and held them out to Chase. He looked surprised, but he reached out and took one. He obviously liked it, because he grabbed another one and ate it as well.

After lunch, he walked with me to my math class, which surprised me. He hadn't done that before. He stopped with me at the door and handed me my bag, holding my crutches while I got it settled on my back. Then he walked off to his next class. I watched his retreating form for a moment, slightly confused by his change in attitude today, but then I shook it off and went into my classroom.

That evening, I overheard my parents talking in the kitchen. I had left my room to get a snack when I heard them talking and stopped to listen.

"I don't know what to do anymore Paul," my mom said. "It's been six months since the accident and she still barely talks."

I heard my dad blow out a breath. "I don't think we can really comprehend what it's like for her, Sandra. Luke wasn't just her brother; he was her twin. You know that the two of them couldn't be apart for more than a couple of days without becoming ill. They were truly part of each other."

"What can we do to help her? I hate seeing her suffer so much. She won't even go out to see the horses. Should we make her see a counselor again?"

"What will that honestly do? You know she'll just sit there and not say anything like she did the few times before that we tried. She just needs time dear."

"She's all we have left Paul. I don't want to lose her too," my mother said brokenly.

I went back to my room after that, and I laid on my bed for a long time, thinking about what they'd said. Was my mother really afraid of losing me? I had contemplated suicide briefly after I had woken up from my coma, but I knew Luke would never forgive me for doing that, so I wasn't going anywhere.

Suddenly it felt like there was someone else in the room. I sat up and looked around, but I didn't see anyone. I started to shrug it off, but then an odd sensation came over me. It was as if something was tugging at my soul, and I grabbed a sweater and my crutches and left the room, following the direction it felt like I was supposed to go.

The feeling took me outside and I soon found myself at the stables for the first time since the accident. I hesitated outside the door for a moment, but the feeling became stronger, so I went into the building. Immediately the familiar scents surrounded me and I felt a sense of homecoming.

Once more I felt the pulling sensation and it brought me to a stall near the end of the aisle. When I looked into the dim interior, my heart clenched. Inside was Justice, Luke's horse. Luke had had him since he was a three-year-old and had trained him on his own.

Justice came to the front of the stall and stuck his head over the door. He dropped his nose onto my shoulder and sighed deeply. I was more than a little shocked. Justice had never been an affectionate horse in the past, but here he was, acting like a little puppy.

It was then that I understood what the tugging sensation had been. "You want me to look after your horse, don't you little brother?" A non-existent breeze ruffled my hair like my brother had always done and tears filled my eyes. "I'll take care of him Luke. I promise."

As soon as I said the words, the feeling disappeared and the tears escaped my eyes. For the first time since I woke up, all the pent up sorrow and anger came out in a flood and I wrapped my arms around Justice's neck and buried my face in his mane. Justice stood completely still while the emotions poured out of me

When the tears had subsided, I released my hold on Justice and moved back a little. "You miss him too, don't you boy? I didn't even think about that when I refused to come down here. But don't worry; I'll come down here every night from now on. It'll be after everyone else has gone to bed, because I don't want anyone knowing that I'm coming here. They'll take it as a sign that I'm ready to start talking to them, and I'm not." I paused for a moment. "That's the most I've spoken in a long time," I finished softly.

Justice snorted and nudged my shoulder gently. "I know, I know. I should have brought you some treats. I will tomorrow," I promised him. "But for now, I'm going to go back up to the house. I'll see you tomorrow."

I left the stables and went back into the house. I forgot to take my sleeping pills, but instead of having nightmares, I dreamt of times my brother and I had gone riding on the trails together. They were happy memories, and when I woke up the next morning, I was surprised to notice that I felt a tiny bit less empty than I had the night before.

When I went into the kitchen for breakfast, my parents were both up already. I hesitated for a moment and then decided I needed to start making a bit of an effort. "Good morning," I murmured.

Both of my parents looked up in surprise, not used to me speaking without prompting. My dad recovered from the shock first. "Good morning Dana. Did you sleep well?"

I nodded and went about getting myself a bowl of cereal. I could see my mom almost sitting on her hands so that she didn't offer to help me. She knew I wanted to be able to do everything on my own. It took me a little longer than it used to, but eventually I managed to sit down and eat my breakfast.

On the way to school, my dad turned to look at me briefly. "How are you doing, Dana? And I want the truth."

I sighed and looked out the window. How was I doing? I still felt like there was a huge hole in me, and my weakened leg irritated me constantly. I hated having to rely on the crutches, but I hated my physical therapy even more. I was about to tell my dad that nothing had changed, but then I thought about Chase, and about my encounter with Justice last night. I was silent for another moment as I wondered if nothing really had changed. Finally, I answered him. "Better."

He let out a relieved breath. "Good."

That was all he said, and I was grateful to him for that. He dropped me off at the front of the school as usual. "See you after school."

I nodded and hobbled into the school. When I got to my first class, I stopped when I saw Adam sitting near the desk I usually sat at. I stood in the doorway for a moment, not entirely sure what to do. A hand touching my back lightly caused me to turn around, and I saw Chase standing behind me, one hand gently encouraging me to enter the room. I reluctantly went to my seat and sat down, refusing to look at Adam as I settled myself.

I was aware of Chase sitting next to me as usual, but I didn't look over at him. I wasn't sure if I was pleased with him encouraging me to come in here when I knew Adam was going to try and talk to me.

I heard Adam shift slightly and then he laid his hand over top of mine. I pulled my hand away from him and he sighed and ducked his head so that I was forced to look at him. "Dana, why won't you talk to me?"

What was I supposed to say to him? I couldn't explain that I couldn't talk to him because he'd sort of been friends with Luke, and the memories of the three of us were too painful to think about. I couldn't tell him that the fact he gave up on me so easily had hurt me when I hadn't thought it would. And I couldn't tell him that the last text he had sent me on that fateful night was the last thing I saw before I had turned to Luke. It was completely irrational, but I now associated Adam's love for me with the accident.

I shook my head and turned my head away from him. I heard sudden movement and then a curse, which had me turning my head back quickly. My eyes widened when I saw that Chase had a hold of Adam's wrist and he was glaring at Adam with the same look he'd had on my second day back.

Adam's jaw was tense as he yanked his hand away from Chase. "This isn't any of your damn business," he snapped.

Chase sat back in his chair without saying anything. He regarded Adam with contempt, but the scary look had left his eyes. When his gaze flickered over to me, he gave me a small smile and then he looked down at the binder in front of him.

When I looked back at Adam, he was watching us in confusion. "What's going on between you two?" When I shrugged, he looked a little hurt. "Have you replaced me with him?"

I was a little startled at his words, and I glanced over at Chase. He was still looking at his binder, but I knew he was also paying attention to what was happening between me and Adam. I knew he wasn't going to be any help, so I decided to just not answer Adam. Instead, I got my own binder out of my bag and pretended to be looking for a piece of paper in in.

The bell rang and I sighed in relief when Adam finally went back to his own seat and Cindy took her seat in front of me. "What was that about?" she asked.

I shrugged and looked at Chase once more. This time he met my look, but I couldn't tell what he was thinking. Deciding that my brain had already taken in too much this morning, I laid my head down on my desk and proceeded to not move for the rest of the class.

# Chapter 5

I ran the brush slowly down Justice's side. My crutches were propped against the stall wall and I was using Justice to keep me upright. It was a very slow process, but Justice was patient with me and he didn't move. This was the fourth night that I'd come down to the stables, but it was the first time I'd tried brushing him.

I patted him and then cautiously ducked under his neck so I could brush his other side, continuing the story I was telling him as I did so. "I haven't heard Chase speak since he said thanks to the teacher. I haven't spoken to him yet, but I think I might soon. I have a feeling that I would be able to talk to him without worrying about him asking me about things that I don't want to talk about."

I hobbled back to the grooming kit and grabbed another brush. "Adam hasn't tried to talk to me since Chase grabbed his wrist. I'm not entirely sure what that was about, but I'm guessing Adam was going to put his hand on my shoulder or something and Chase stopped him." I paused for a moment. "I wonder why he did that," I murmured and then shrugged it off. "I'm sure he has his reasons. I sometimes wonder what his story is. I know he lives with foster parents, but that's about it. Maybe one day I'll find out, but I'm not going to push him."

I fell silent and finished brushing him, then grabbed my crutches. I gave Justice a last pat before I let myself out of the stall. "I'll see you tomorrow night boy." I put the grooming kit back in the tack room and then left the building to head back up to the house.

Once back inside, I changed into my pajamas and crawled under my covers without taking my sleeping pills once again. I hadn't taken them all week and the nightmares hadn't bothered me. I hadn't told my parents yet that I'd stopped taking them, but I was planning on telling them soon.

When I woke up the next morning, my leg was feeling better than it had since the accident. As I made my way into the kitchen, I decided that it must be partially because of the extra exercise that I'd been getting every night by going down to the stables. My physical therapist was constantly telling me that exercise would make my leg stronger, but I'd never really listened to her, since I had no desire to strengthen it. But now that I had promised Luke that I would look after his horse, maybe I should actually concentrate on my physical therapy a little more.

I greeted my parents when I got to the kitchen. They stopped talking when I came in, which instantly made me suspicious. I made myself a bowl of cereal and sat at the table, knowing that if they wanted to tell me what they were talking about, they would. I ate my breakfast quietly and once I'd put my bow in the sink, my dad finally told me what they'd been talking about. "Dana, can you sit down for a moment?"

I sat back down at the table and looked at him expectantly. He blew out a breath and glanced at my mother before speaking again. "We were thinking of selling Destiny."

I was a little surprised at his words. They wanted to sell Destiny? I was quiet for a moment as I thought about how that made me feel. I'd only had her for about three months before the accident, so I hadn't had time to form too much of a bond with her. I'd always enjoyed riding her, but I knew that it wasn't fair to keep her when I wasn't doing anything with her. I looked at my dad and shrugged. "Okay."

Both of my parents let out little sighs of relief. "Good, we already have a prospective buyer for her. We just didn't want to make a final decision until we'd talked to you."

I nodded, grateful that they'd spoken to me even though I hadn't shown any interest in the horses since I was in the hospital. A sudden thought had me tensing up. "What about Justice?"

My dad looked shocked that I'd asked him that, but he answered me anyways. "We wouldn't be able to sell him even if we wanted to." When I looked at him questioningly, he explained. "Justice won't perform for anyone since Luke died. He can be ridden, but he knocks over even the smallest jumps. He just doesn't show interest in anything anymore."

I raised my eyebrows. Justice had always loved jumping, and he used to clear everything by at least a foot to make sure he didn't knock any of them down. And what did my dad mean when he said Justice didn't show interest in anything? He was always very happy to see me, nickering at me as soon as I entered the building. I didn't tell my parents that, though.

If I did, they'd know that I'd been spending time at the barn. So I didn't say anything; instead I just stood up and got ready for school.

Chase was waiting for me outside of our first class. I cocked my head at him questioningly, but he didn't say anything as he followed me into the room and we took our seats. We spent the class like we always did, and parted ways afterwards. Cindy and Sarah had a yearbook meeting at lunch again, so we sat alone at the cafeteria. It felt like something had changed between us, but I wasn't entirely sure what it was.

At the end of our English class, he handed me a piece of paper. I frowned as I took it and unfolded it. A phone number was written on it, and I raised startled eyes up to Chase. He was regarding me with expressionless eyes, so I had no idea what giving me his number meant to him. I pulled my phone out of my pocket and entered his name and number into my contacts. Then I sent him a blank text message so that he'd have my number as well.

A tiny smile touched his lips as he pulled his phone out his own pocket and stored my number. When he looked at me again, his expression had warmed and he cautiously reached up and touched my cheek briefly. My eyes widened at the contact, but before I could react he had grabbed my bag for me and started leaving the room. I followed along behind him, struggling to figure out what this all meant.

Once at my locker, he handed my bag back to me and turned to leave. I reached out and touched his arm lightly, causing him to freeze and then slowly turn back to face me. "Bye," I said quietly, uttering my first word to him.

His eyes lit up, catching me off guard. It suddenly struck me that he was really good-looking. He touched my cheek once more, his fingers lingering for a moment longer than earlier. "Bye," he whispered, and then he left.

I raised a hand to my cheek, marveling in the warmth I had felt from his touch. Then I blew out a breath and headed out to the parking lot, where I knew Cindy would be waiting for me.

On Sunday afternoon, I sat on the couch in the living room and stared down at my phone. I had Chase's number on the screen, and I was debating what to do with it. I couldn't call him; that would be entirely too awkward. But could I send him a text?

After another fifteen minutes of indecision, I finally decided to leave it for now. We had spoken our first words to each other only two days ago. Texting him felt like it would be too much right now. I put my phone down and picked up the book that I had been reading.

My mom came in a few minutes later and sat down next to me. "Good book?" When I nodded, she smiled. "Want to help me make supper?"

I was surprised at her request. Since I'd come home, my mom had gotten into the habit of trying to do a lot of things for me. I knew she was only trying to help, but it annoyed me to be treated like a child. The fact that she was asking me to help her make dinner showed me that maybe she was trying to make more of an effort not to suffocate me. I used to always help her with meals, and I'd always enjoyed the strictly mother/daughter time.

I nodded once more and her whole face lit up. "Great! I was thinking we could make lasagna, since it's your dad's favorite."

I followed her into the kitchen and we set about making dinner together. It was surprisingly easy to get back into our normal routine and I found myself relaxing and almost enjoying myself. When my dad came in he blinked a couple of times when he found me in the kitchen, but then he grinned hugely. "Something smells good," he stated as he crossed to my mom and kissed her cheek.

"We're making lasagna," she replied happily.

"I'd better go have a shower quickly then. I don't want to miss my favorite meal." He left the kitchen, and my mother and I finished making supper.

It still felt weird sitting at the table to eat without Luke there, but I was slowly getting used to it. I no longer looked around the kitchen as I sat down, half expecting him to appear around the corner.

When I went down to see Justice later that night, I sat down in his stall with my back resting against the wall. My left leg was stretched out in front of me, and my right foot was on the ground with my knee bent. Justice was standing on my right side with his head lowered, his nose nearly touching my knee as I ran my fingers through his forelock. "I helped my mom make dinner tonight."

Justice sighed and lowered his head the last few inches so that his muzzle was now resting on my leg. His eyes were half closed as he obviously enjoyed my attention. "I feel guilty for trying to go on with my life without Luke here with me. I know he would want me to move on, but it feels wrong somehow. As if I'm betraying him or something."

I was quiet for a few minutes as I thought about it, and then I changed the subject. "My leg is getting stronger. I went for physical therapy yesterday and my therapist commented that it seemed to be getting better. I think it has to do with the fact that I'm exercising it more by coming down here at night." I stopped petting him so I could reach forward and roll the left leg of my jeans up. I examined the mass of scars that marred the skin from my knee to my ankle. "It's not pretty to look at, is it?" I murmured.

Justice nudged my shoulder with his nose, so I rolled my pant leg back down and started petting him again. "You don't care what it looks like, do you? You just want me to keep paying attention to you." I hand my hand over his silky nose. "You know, my dad told me the other day that you aren't performing anymore. Why is that? You always loved jumping before. I guess it's good in a way, since it means they won't sell you, but I think you should try and perform a little better. What would Luke think if he saw all his hard work of training you going down the drain?"

It hit me then that I should be telling myself the same thing as well. What would Luke say if he saw the person I'd become? He'd probably scold me and then annoy me until I started making an effort again. Whenever I'd become discouraged about something before, that's what he'd done. I'd done the same to him as well.

I knew in my heart that Luke would be angry with me if he saw me today. But I wasn't able to really do anything about it yet. Maybe one day I'd be strong enough to be the person I was before the accident, but I didn't know when that day would be, if it even happened.

With a sigh, I struggled to my feet and settled my crutches under my arms. "Life can be so hard sometimes, Justice. I don't know how I'm going to get through the rest of it without him." When Justice shuffled closer to me, I laid my forehead against his. "I'm so glad I have you to talk to. I'll see you tomorrow."

# Chapter 6

The cafeteria was crowded when Chase and I entered it on Tuesday afternoon. Cindy had saved seats for us like she usually did, so we headed in that direction. When I spotted Adam sitting by himself, staring out the window, I hesitated for a moment. After my talk with Justice on Sunday, I'd done some thinking about Adam.

Chase turned to see why I had paused, and he followed my gaze. Something flickered in his eyes, but it was gone too quickly for me to identify what the emotion had been. He looked back at me, clearly waiting for me to decide what to do.

I was torn. I felt bad about how I'd been treating Adam, but I wasn't sure if I was ready to talk to him about it. Reaching a decision, I headed over to where he was sitting, aware that Chase was following behind me. Adam glanced up when I stopped near him and surprise registered on his face. "Dana?"

I couldn't look at him, so I stared at my hands as I spoke. "I'm sorry," I muttered quietly.

I heard him get to his feet, and I scooted back a few steps, colliding into Chase. He placed his hands on my hips for a moment to keep me from falling and then he released me. I raised my head to look at Adam and saw that he was watching me closely. "What are you sorry for?" he asked.

I blew out a shuddering breath and closed my eyes briefly. "Everything," I replied, and then turned and made my way out of the cafeteria as quickly as I could, ignoring Adam as he called after me. I wasn't capable of saying anything else to him; those three words had been hard enough.

For some reason, I went up the stairs that were close to the cafeteria. I hadn't been on the second floor of the school since I'd come back; all my classes were on the first floor to make it easier on my leg. The hallway was silent, with only the tapping of my crutches breaking the stillness as I moved forward. When I saw the decorated locker, I came to an abrupt halt. In my preoccupation with getting away from Adam, I'd inadvertently ended up in front of Luke's old locker.

I stared at the paper that covered the door. There were hundreds of little messages and signatures covering it, along with photos of my brother. Someone had taped a flower to it, and it was fresh so I knew someone had done it recently. I hobbled a few steps closer to look at the photos and my breath hitched when I saw one of Luke and I that had been taken only a few days before the accident.

In the picture, Luke had his arm slung around my shoulders with a big grin on his face. We both had our faces painted in the school colors of royal blue and silver, since it was the day of the pep rally. I was laughing as I looked into the camera, but I couldn't remember what had been so funny.

I sensed rather than heard someone behind me. I didn't have to turn around to know that it was Chase. "That's my brother," I murmured.

Chase moved to stand beside me. "He looks happy," he replied.

A small smile touched my lips. "He was always happy. It used to annoy me that he always had a smile on his face and nothing bothered him. Nothing I did would make him mad."

Chase reached up and brushed a piece of hair off my face. "You were close to him?"

My chest tightened as I nodded. "Very."

He turned to look at the paper again and I knew he was reading some of the messages that had been left. After a few minutes, he glanced at me again. "It looks like he was well loved."

"It was impossible not to like him." I blinked suddenly. "Hey, we're talking."

Chase seemed mildly startled when he realized that. "I guess we are."

We both fell silent after that, which I found very amusing. When I looked at Chase, I saw that he was fighting not to smile as well. I bumped him lightly with my shoulder. "Come on, let's go back down."

I felt strangely lighter as the day went on. I'd talked about Luke for the first time, and it hadn't been as difficult as I'd thought it was going to be. Chase and I didn't speak again for the rest of the day, but I sensed a lightness in him as well that hadn't been there before.

When I brushed Justice that night, I told him about the conversation I'd had with Chase. "I didn't think I'd ever be able to talk about Luke again, but it wasn't too hard talking to Chase. It was strange how we just suddenly started talking to each other. I'm more comfortable with him than I am with anyone else."

When I settled myself in bed that night, I thought about what had happened that day. I'd made my first attempt to talk to Adam, and it had gone better than I'd expected it to. I'd seen Luke's old locker and it had caught me off guard, but in the end it had made me realize how much everyone missed him. And I'd had an actual conversation with Chase, though it had been fairly short. All in all, I decided it had been a good day and I fell asleep with a small smile on my lips.

The next morning, my parents were oddly silent at breakfast, and they kept sending me uncertain looks. I had no idea what was going on, and I quickly decided that I didn't want to know. It obviously wasn't anything good, and I didn't want to spoil the new lightness that had come into my life yesterday.

When I got to my first class at school, both Cindy and Adam sent me searching looks and I started to get slightly annoyed. Chase didn't say anything as we waited for the bell to ring, and for that I was grateful. Despite my best intentions, my good mood was slipping away, and I concentrated on my binder, randomly doodling until the teacher called the class to attention by announcing we were having a pop quiz.

It wasn't until I went to write the date at the top of my test paper that I realized why everyone had been acting oddly today. I froze in place as I stared down at the paper. How could I forget? I wondered bewilderedly. I knew that I'd been in a funk for the last six months, but how had I forgotten that it was my birthday?

It suddenly felt as if the room was closing in on me. My breathing picked up, and before I fully registered what I was doing, I scrambled to my feet. I glanced around the room and saw everyone looking at me in surprise. Both Cindy and Adam looked sympathetic, but I couldn't deal with them. I couldn't deal with anyone. I grabbed my crutches and left as fast as I possibly could. I heard chairs scraping across the floor behind me, but I couldn't stop. I also heard Cindy's voice shouting something, but I didn't hear what it was.

I moved faster than I thought was possible and less than a minute later I was bursting out of the school. The cold air slammed into me as I crossed the parking lot, finally stopping at the park that was at the end. I made my way to a bench and collapsed onto it, ignoring my crutches as they clattered onto the frozen ground. I rested my elbows on my knees and cradled my head in my hands.

Someone sat down next to me, and an arm went around my shoulders. Just like yesterday, I knew it was Chase without looking up. My breathing hitched, and his arm tightened around me. I lifted my head from my hands and looked over at him. His eyes were full of compassion, though I knew he had no idea what had suddenly upset me. I laid my head on his shoulder and pressed my face into the crook of his neck as tears started coursing down my cheeks. I cried silently, taking comfort in his warmth and in his silence.

When I managed to compose myself, I remained still for a moment before lifting my head again and looking down at my hands. "It's my birthday," I whispered. I saw Chase looking at me quizzically from the corner of my eye, so I continued. "Luke..." I swallowed hard and took a couple of deep breaths. "Luke was my twin," I finished hoarsely.

Chase raised the arm that wasn't around me and gently brushed the tears off my cheeks. "You didn't tell me that yesterday," he said.

"It's hard for me to talk about him," I replied.

He nodded. "I know what you mean. I lost my parents when I was ten."

The unexpected information caused me to look over at him again. "How do you get over something like this?"

He sighed and placed his one hand back in his lap, but he didn't remove his arm from around my shoulders. "You don't get over it. You just learn to live with it and you try to move on."

I let out a shaky breath. "I don't know how I could have forgotten that it was my birthday today."

Chase was silent for a moment. "When did your brother die?" he asked gently.

"Just over six months ago. We were in a car accident." When his gaze strayed to my left leg, I nodded. "That's how I was injured."

Chase didn't say anything else; he just sat next to me quietly for the next fifteen minutes. Finally, he stood up and held his hand down to me. "Come on, let's get out of here."

"Where are we going?" I asked as I let him help me to my feet and hand me my crutches.

"Where do you want to go? It's your birthday."

I thought about it for a moment. "I want to go visit my brother's grave. I haven't been there yet."

Chase nodded and I followed him back into the school parking lot. He surprised me when he led me over to a car. "I didn't know you had a car."

His lips twisted into something resembling a sneer. "These foster parents have a lot of money," he said bitterly.

I wanted to ask him what he meant by that, but I held my tongue. I'd already learned one thing about him today and I wasn't going to try and learn anything else. He helped me get into the car and then I gave him directions to the cemetery.

Once there, I didn't need directions to my brother's grave. I knew instinctively where it was, and I headed straight for it. I stared down at the headstone, not knowing what to say. I placed a hand on the cool marble and struggled to keep my tears at bay. "Happy eighteenth birthday, little brother. I miss you more than you could ever imagine." I wanted to say more, but the words got stuck in my throat, and I found it difficult to breathe all of a sudden.

Chase slid his arms around my waist from behind me and pulled me close until my back was pressed against his chest. I was surprised at first, but then I relaxed into him and my breathing slowly returned to normal. The closeness of him gave me the strength to say one last thing to my brother. "Good bye, Luke. I love you."

Chase and I walked back to the car and I told him how to get to my place. When we were sitting in the driveway, I turned to him. "Thank you."

"You're welcome. Will you be okay here?"

I nodded. "My parents are home; they're just down at the stables right now. They'll come back to the house shortly."

"You have my number if you need me."

I gave him a small smile. "I know. I'll see you at school tomorrow, okay?"

"Okay."

I got out of the car and headed into the house, turning once to wave as Chase pulled away. Once I was inside, I went into the bathroom and started running a bath for myself. My parents came in while the water was running, and neither of them seemed too surprised to see me. "Are you okay?" my mom asked.

I shook my head. "No, but I will be."

This seemed to satisfy them both, because they left me to myself after that. I soaked in the tub for an hour and then decided to have a nap. I could barely eat anything at supper that night, but my parents understood and didn't comment on it.

That night, I went down to the barn as usual. Justice was waiting for me and I instantly wrapped my arms around his neck and hugged him tightly. "It was our birthday today, Justice. I miss him so much."

Justice craned his neck until it felt like he was almost hugging me back, and I felt comforted. When I released my hold on him, I looked at him thoughtfully. "I just had a really bad idea," I told him. "Wait here."

I went to the tack room and clumsily grabbed a saddle, saddle pad and girth. I slowly made my way back down the aisle, trying to balance the awkward load without tripping on my crutches. I got back to the stall and let myself in. Justice stood patiently while I put the saddle pad and saddle on him, and he didn't flinch when I tightened the girth. I went back down to the tack room and put on a helmet before grabbing his bridle and going to his stall once more.

When he was fully tacked up, I put both my crutches under one are and led him out of the stall to the indoor arena. I was immensely grateful that my parents always left low lights on throughout the building. It didn't make it very bright, but it was enough that I could see without running into anything.

We went into the arena and I positioned him by the mounting block. I bit my lip as I studied the mounting block. "Try not to move," I murmured as I set my crutches down and pulled myself up the two steps. I leaned against Justice for a moment, gathering up my courage. Then I managed to pull myself onto him with a lot less effort than I thought it would take. Once I was on him, I just sat there for a minute.

When I was comfortable, I gathered up my reins and nudged him into a walk. Justice immediately moved out, striding around the arena with his ears pricked alertly. I was a little worried that he would spook at the dimness of the arena, but he moved confidently without faltering once.

As we walked around, a smile started to form on my face. By the time we had gone around five times, I was smiling fully for the first time. After another two circuits, I decided that it was enough and guided him back to the mounting block. He once again stood completely still while I slowly wiggled my way off of him. Once I was firmly on the ground once more, I threw my arms around his neck for another hug. "That was a birthday gift for both of us, Luke," I whispered and then turned to put Justice away.

# Chapter 7

Two weeks went by, and I rode Justice almost every night. I never did anything more than walking, but it still felt really good to be riding again. Justice seemed to enjoy it as well; he was always eager and alert when I rode him around. My leg became stronger with each passing day, and my physical therapist was optimistic about me being able to graduate to a cane shortly, which would give me more freedom.

Chase and I continued to talk a little, but only when there wasn't anyone else around. It was an unspoken agreement between us that we didn't really want anyone else at the school to know that we talked to each other. He didn't tell me anything else about his past, but we discovered that we had similar tastes in music and movies. I noticed that he seemed to enjoy touching me in small ways, but he never did anything that made me uncomfortable. He just had a habit of touching my cheek or my arm when we were talking.

On a Friday afternoon, he surprised me by offering to give me a ride home. Aside from my birthday, we hadn't done anything together outside of school. I agreed though, and let

Cindy know. I know she was surprised, but I think she was also happy that I was getting so close to Chase.

Chase drove me to my house, and once we were there I turned to him. "Do you want to come in for a few minutes?"

I saw him debate internally about it, and then he finally nodded. "Sure."

We got out of his car and went into the house. My parents weren't in yet, which wasn't unusual. Now that winter had made an appearance, there was more work to be done down at the stables. I led Chase into the kitchen. "Want a hot chocolate?" When he nodded, I set about making us both a cup and then sat down across from him at the table.

We sat quietly for a few minutes as we sipped on our drinks. Finally, Chase looked over at me. "This is a nice place."

I smiled slightly. "I've always liked it."

"Have you always lived here?"

I nodded. "Yeah, this is the only home I've ever known."

He stared into his mug of hot chocolate for a moment. "Before my parents died, I only ever had one home as well," he said quietly.

My eyes raised to meet his and I saw the pain in them. "How did they die?" I asked softly.

"Plane crash," he replied. "It was a small plane with only ten passengers on it."

"Where were you?"

"At home. My parents had planned to go on a short holiday for their anniversary, so I stayed with a friend of theirs. It would have been there first vacation together."

My heart went out to him, and I reached across the table to place my hand on his, but I didn't say anything. There was nothing that could be said.

The sounds of my parents coming in interrupted our silence, and I withdrew my hand from his as my dad came into the kitchen. He stopped short when he saw that I wasn't alone. "Hello," he said, his curiosity evident.

"Dad, this is Chase. Chase, that's my dad." As I made the introductions, my mom came in. "And that's my mom."

"It's nice to meet you, Chase," my dad said, though I could tell he was a little confused as to why there was a strange boy in the house.

"You too," Chase mumbled before standing up and looking at me. "I should go."

"Would you like to stay for dinner?" my mom asked.

Chase shook his head. "I can't, but thanks."

I got to my feet and followed him to the front door. He stopped there and turned to face me. "I've never talked to anyone about my parents before," he murmured.

"Just like I haven't talked to anyone else about Luke," I replied in a quiet voice. "What does that say about us?"

He shrugged and then gave me a shy smile. "I have no idea, but I like being around you."

I returned his smile. "I like being around you too," I said honestly. It was true; for some reason he was the only person I felt completely comfortable with.

Chase hesitated for a moment and then shocked me by leaning down and kissing my cheek lightly. When he straightened up again, his cheeks were slightly red. "I'll see you on Monday," he said and then left the house.

I was too stunned to move for a few minutes as I watched him through the window beside the door. He got into his car and drove away, and when he was out of sight I was finally able to make myself move again. I went back into the kitchen and found my parents looking at me expectantly. "What?"

My mom gave me an amused smile. "What do you think? Who was that boy?"

I sighed and sat down in the chair I had vacated earlier. "A friend from school."

"He's the first person we've seen you interact with since the accident, aside from Cindy. You have to expect us to be curious," my dad said.

I put my elbows on the table and rested my chin on top of my hands. "I can talk to him," I replied quietly.

"About Luke?"

I nodded. "He hasn't had an easy life, so he understands without making me uncomfortable or pushing me into talking if I don't want to."

My dad blew out a breath and sat down beside me. "Is that why you won't talk to us? Because you're worried we'll try and get you to talk more than you're ready to?" When I nodded, he patted my shoulder. "I can understand that, but if you do want to talk about anything, we're both here for you and we'll try not to push you into anything. Okay?"

I nodded again and looked down at the table. "I went to Luke's grave."

Both my parents inhaled sharply, but they didn't say anything and I found myself relaxing slightly when I realized they really meant it about trying not to push me. I looked up at my mom and then at my dad. "I went on my birthday. Chase took me there and then brought me home."

My dad put his arm around my shoulders. "I don't know Chase, but I'm already grateful to him for helping you when we couldn't. He's welcome here anytime."

I smiled at both of them. "Thanks. Don't be offended that he didn't stay; apparently I'm the only person he's willingly talked to since school started." I decided to change the subject. "So, what's for dinner?"

"Well Dana, I think it's safe to say that you can now move onto a cane. Your leg has gotten a lot stronger in the past month or so," Jared, my physical therapist, informed me. He sat down on a chair and smiled at me. "I don't know what's changed since I first started seeing you, but keep it up."

"I'll try," I replied, getting to my feet and preparing to leave.

"Dana," Jared said hesitantly, and when I turned to look at him again, I saw that he was frowning thoughtfully. "I don't normally do this, but I thought maybe you'd like to meet someone I know. She's like a little sister to me, and she was in a car accident a few years ago that killed her parents and put her brother into a coma. Her brother has since woken up, but it took a long time for that to happen. Hailey suffers with serious back problems, but she's one of the most amazing people I've ever known. It might do you some good to talk to her, since she knows a little about what you went through."

I was surprised that he had said anything like that. I hadn't exactly always been the best patient, and I hadn't expected him to offer me any kind of extra help. "I'll think about it. Thanks."

He grinned. "No problem. I think you'd like her, though she is a few years older than you."

I thought about his words as my dad drove me home from the appointment. Maybe I would take Jared up on his offer and meet this girl one day. I hadn't spoken to anyone else who had a serious injury. I wondered if it would help to talk to someone who had suffered physically as well.

Before riding Justice that night, I grabbed my phone and scrolled down to Chase's number. I selected it, hesitated a moment, and then sent him a quick text.

Moving onto a cane- D

A few minutes later, I got a text back from him.

That's great- C

I smiled, happy that he had replied to me, and then set down my phone. I went down to the barn and rode Justice, and when I got back to the house, I saw that I had another text from Chase that he had sent ten minutes ago.

Good night- C

I sent him one back saying the same thing, and then crawled into bed to get some sleep.

On Monday morning, I was using my cane for the first time when I got to the school. I had practiced using it home yesterday, so I had the hang of it already. Chase was waiting for me at my locker, and he smiled slightly when he saw me. He took my bag for me while I opened my locker and then he placed it in there for me and grabbed my binder before shutting the door. We walked to our classroom together and sat in our usual seats.

Cindy came in and her eyes lit up when she saw that I had a cane instead of crutches. "Hey, you're moving up in the world," she said teasingly.

I rolled my eyes and shook my head at her, choosing not to say anything as there were too many people in the room. She grinned at me and then took her seat. I looked over at Chase and saw that he had an amused expression on his face as he looked between me and Cindy. When he caught my eye, I smiled slightly at him before turning to pay attention to the teacher.

After school, Chase once again offered to drive me home. I agreed and when we were in the car, I glanced at him. "Is this going to be a regular thing now?"

His eyes flickered to mine before turning back to the road. "If you want it to be."

I nodded. "I'd like that."

He didn't say anything else until we got to my place and I started to get out of the car. "Dana," he said softly. When I turned to look at him, he wouldn't meet my eyes. "Would you like to go out with me sometime?"

I sat back in my seat and nibbled on my lip for a moment as I thought about it. I wasn't sure what my feelings were when it came to Chase, but I did know that I wanted to see more of him. "Sure, that would be nice."

A huge smile split his face. "Great, maybe we can go out tomorrow after school."

"Sounds good." I hesitated a moment, and then leaned over and kissed his cheek. "See you tomorrow."

# Chapter 8

Chase picked me up at six the next evening, and I found that I was really looking forward to going out with him. I hadn't asked him where we were going, since it didn't really matter to me. I knew he'd find something that we would both enjoy.

When he arrived at my house, my stomach fluttered a little, surprising me. I hadn't felt anything like that since Adam and I started dating nearly two years ago. I told my parents I was leaving and then went outside to get into the car. Chase smile briefly at me when I got in, and then he started driving.

We drove for about twenty minutes before he pulled into a parking lot. When I saw where we were, I turned to him with a smile. "Canada's national pastime?"

He grinned shyly back. "I remember you saying you were a hockey fan. I thought it would be fun for us to watch the local team play."

"I think you're right. Let's go in."

We walked into the arena, and then Chase surprised me by going to the elevator. "My foster parents had tickets for a sky box," he explained. "They weren't able to make it tonight, so they asked if I wanted the tickets. I'm pretty sure I shocked them when I actually said yes," he said with a wry smile.

"My parents were very surprised when I told them I was going out tonight," I admitted as we arrived at our assigned box and took our seats. "But I also know they were pleased. I haven't gone out anywhere for fun since the accident."

He placed his hand over mine and squeezed it gently. "I'm glad you wanted to come out with me."

I smiled at him. "Me too."

We didn't talk too much during the game. A couple of servers checked on us a few times to see if we needed anything, but other than that we were left alone. I'd never been in a sky box before, but it was kind of nice not having to jostle around people to get what we wanted. I knew with my cane that it would've been fairly difficult to do that, so I was grateful for the relative privacy that we had.

Our team won and I found myself cheering for them along with the rest of the crowd. Chase watched me with an amused expression, but even he got into the spirit of things at the final goal. When it was over, we made our way back to the car. We managed to beat the rush out of the parking lot, and soon we were heading back to my place.

Most of the lights were off at my house when we got there, and I knew my parents were in bed already. I hesitated for a moment before getting out of the car. I turned and leaned back in to look at Chase. "Come with me. I want to show you something."

He followed me down the driveway to the stables and into the building. I led him over to where Justice was waiting with his head over the stall door. "This is Justice. He was Luke's horse."

Chase eyed the horse warily. "He's pretty big."

I raised an eyebrow. "Don't tell me you're afraid of horses."

"I'm not. I just have a healthy respect for anything that's big enough to eat me."

I laughed and grabbed his hand, pulling him closer. "Justice won't hurt you. He's a good boy."

Chase cautiously reached his hand out and stroked Justice's nose. "He's soft," he murmured.

"Can I tell you a secret?" I asked him.

He turned his eyes to me. "Sure."

"I've been coming out here and riding him every night for the past couple of weeks. Luke trained him on his own, so it helps me feel closer to him when I spend time with Justice. No one else knows that I come down here. They all think I haven't been near a horse since the accident."

"Why don't you tell them what you've been doing?"

I sighed and leaned back against the stall door. "If I do, my parents will think I'm all better and they'll start pushing me to do other things again. I'm not ready for anything else yet. Right now, this is my escape. If everyone knows about it, it no longer will be."

He nodded. "I know what you mean. Running is my escape."

I tilted my head slightly. "You run?"

"Yeah. Every morning and most evenings as well. I've been doing it since I was thirteen." A haunted expression came over his face for a moment before it went blank.

"Are you fast?"

His lips turned up slightly. "Yeah, I'm pretty fast."

Satisfied that I'd snapped him out of the thoughts that had distressed him, I turned back to Justice. "I'm too tired to ride tonight, but I wanted you to see him."

Chase brushed the back of his hand down my cheek. "Thanks."

"You're welcome." We stayed there for another minute before walking up to the house. At the front door, I turned to him. "I had fun tonight."

"So did I," he replied. "Do you want to go out again sometime?"

I bit my lip and looked down at the ground. "Yes, but I need to talk to Adam first."

Chase inhaled sharply. "I thought you two weren't together."

When I looked back up at him, his face was closed off. "We're not together. But I need to talk to him anyways. I need closure with him, which I don't have yet. I haven't been able to make myself talk to him."

He relaxed visibly. "Okay, I can understand that." He put his arms around me and pulled me into him for a hug. Then he bent his head and brushed his lips very lightly over mine. "I'll see you at school tomorrow."

I put my fingers to my lips and watched as he got in his car and drove away. Then, with a small smile, I went into the house and got ready for bed.

The next day, I waited by the doors of the cafeteria for Adam at lunch time. My stomach was in knots at the thought of having a conversation with him, but I knew I had to do it.

I couldn't let myself have a relationship with Chase until I'd cleared everything up with Adam.

When I spotted Adam coming towards me, I pushed myself off the wall and hobbled toward him. "Can we talk?" I asked him quietly.

Surprise flitted across his features, but he nodded and we went into the cafeteria together. We went to the back and found an empty table that was slightly away from the others. We sat down and he looked at me expectantly. "What's going on?"

I played absently with my fingers as I thought of how to best start the conversation. "Chase took me out last night."

Adam sighed. "I knew it was going to happen eventually."

I looked up at him in surprise. "What do you mean?"

"Dana, anyone who looks at the two of you together can see that there's something going on. It was only a matter of time until you became a couple."

I shook my head. "We're not a couple. We only went out on one date."

"You don't want to go out with him again?"

I blushed slightly and looked down at my hands again. "I didn't say that," I mumbled.

"If you want to go out with him, then why don't you?" He sounded confused.

"I told him I needed to talk to you first," I replied, glancing up at him.

Understanding crossed his features. "Ah, I see. Dana, we haven't really been a couple since... well you know when. I mean, this is the first time we've actually talked in over seven months."

"I know, but I wanted to try and explain why I've avoided you all this time. You didn't do anything wrong and I feel bad that I kept pushing you away."

He reached forward and covered my hands with one of his. "I know why you did. It took me a long time to figure it out, but I finally did. It's because Luke and I were friends, right? Being with me brings back too many memories, doesn't it?"

I nodded. "I'm sorry. I just couldn't do it."

"I get it. I miss him too."

I turned one of my hands over and squeezed his lightly before pulling back. "Maybe we can start over as friends."

"We can try," he said. "And as your friend, I have to ask; how do you and Chase communicate?"

I raised an eyebrow as I sat back and crossed my arms over my chest. "How do you think we communicate? We talk."

"Really? But he never talks."

I rolled my eyes. "Just like I never talk anymore, right?"

He grinned sheepishly. "Right."

"Chase and I don't talk if there's other people around, but if we're alone we talk all the time. Neither of us feels that what we talk about is anyone's business."

Adam tilted his head slightly, obviously surprised at the tone of my voice. "You'll never be the same person that you were before, will you?" he asked softly.

I shook my head. "No, I won't. How can I be when half of me is missing?"

He sighed and ran a hand through his hair. "I hope Chase can help you. I know I can't."

"You're a great guy, Adam. I have no doubt that you'll find a girl that's perfect for you sometime soon. You were right for the girl that I used to be. But I'm too screwed up now to be any good for you. Chase is as screwed up as I am, so we oddly seem to suit each other."

Adam nodded. "I hope he can make you happy." He held out his hand to me. "Friends?"

I accepted his hand and gave him a small smile. "Friends."

After school, Chase and I walked to his car. Once we were on the road, I looked over at him. He knew I'd talked to Adam at lunch, but he hadn't asked me about it and I didn't know how to bring it up. I stayed silent until we reached my house and then I invited him to come in for a few minutes. He agreed and we went inside and into the living room. "I talked to Adam at lunch today," I told him.

"I know."

I looked at him questioningly. "Don't you want to know what we talked about?"

He shrugged. "Only if you want to tell me."

I frowned in confusion. "Did I do something wrong?"

His face was expressionless as he regarded me. "No."

I sighed and leaned back on the couch, a little unsure of what to do. Something was obviously bothering him, but I wasn't sure what it was. So I decided to just tell him about my conversation with Adam. As I spoke, I watched as his face changed, becoming lighter and a smile started tugging at his lips. It suddenly dawned on me that he had thought I was going to reject him. "What did you think was going to happen when I talked to him?"

He lowered his eyes. "I don't know."

"Did you think I was going to get back together with him?"

He looked up at me with a suddenly vulnerable expression. "I'm not used to having good things happen to me," he explained quietly.

My heart went out to him and I scooted closer until I was pressed lightly against his side. He lifted his arm and cautiously placed it over my shoulders, and I smiled at him. "Are you happy?" I asked him.

He nodded. "Yeah." He was quiet for a moment and then he spoke again. "I've never had a girlfriend," he admitted.

"Really?"

"Really. It's kind of hard to have a relationship with a girl when I won't talk to them," he said dryly.

"That would make it difficult," I agreed. "So why do you talk to me?"

"Because you've experienced pain like I have. I recognized that from the first day we met."

I thought back to that day and remembered the recognition I'd felt when my eyes had met his for the first time. "I felt the same way," I replied.

We sat quietly for a few moments before he reluctantly removed his arm from my shoulders and got to his feet. "I should get going home."

"Okay." I struggled to my feet so I could walk with him to the door.

He put his arm around my waist as we maneuvered our way through the house. "Can I pick you up for school tomorrow?" he asked as we reached the front door.

"That would be nice."

He turned to face me and stroked my cheek lightly. "I'll see you tomorrow then." He looked a little unsure for a moment, and then he lowered his head and pressed his lips to mine.

Pleasure rushed through me at the contact, and I responded by sliding one of my arms around his neck. The kiss was soft and very sweet. When he pulled back after a minute, I smiled up at him. "For never having a girlfriend before, you're pretty good at this."

He grinned a little shyly. "I guess I'm a fast learner." He gave me another quick kiss and then turned and left the house.

When I rode Justice that night, I was lost in thought as we ambled around the arena. When he suddenly stopped, I focused on my surroundings and saw that we were now standing in front of a low cross rail that had obviously been set up for a beginner lesson. The middle of the jump was only about a foot high, so I squeezed my legs and Justice carefully picked up each foot as he went over it. I patted his neck and then slid off of him and led him back to his stall. "I think we can start to step up our rides," I informed him as I untacked him. "I want to see if you'll eventually jump for me. I think it'll be awhile before we can attempt that, thought."

I finished untacking him and brushed him down quickly. I gave him a last pat as I shut his stall door. "See you tomorrow night boy."

# Chapter 9

I learned something about Chase on Friday afternoon. The day had gone by as it usually did, but as we got ready to go home for the day, something happened that gave me a little more insight into the mysterious boy that I had become so close to.

We were walking down the hall towards the doors. Chase had my bag slung over his right shoulder, and he was holding my right hand with his left one, as I used my other hand for my cane. As we came to the intersection of two hallways, someone came skidding around the corner and bumped into me. I was knocked off balance a little, but I managed to stay on my feet, though I did have to drop Chase's hand to do so.

Unfortunately, the collision with me had sent the person into a dive, and he desperately grabbed at Chase to try and keep himself from slamming into the ground. He managed to get a hold of Chase's arm, but I think he quickly wished that he hadn't.

Chase's reaction was immediate. His right hand swung forward and slammed into the guy's jaw, causing him to release his grip on Chase's arm immediately. Chase then backed up two quick steps and stood completely still, his hands clenched into tight fists at his sides and his whole body rigid.

I gaped at the boy now sprawled on the ground. It had happened so quickly that it took my brain a moment to realize what had happened. I looked up at Chase and saw that his face was a blank mask. My bag had dropped off his shoulder and was sitting in a heap on the floor by his feet. I glanced around the hallway quickly and was relieved to see that no one had witnessed the little scene, since almost everyone had already left the school.

Using my cane, I nudged the boy on the ground. "Are you okay?" I asked him.

He rolled onto his back and looked up at me dazedly. "I think so," he replied.

I tilted my head slightly. "Sorry I hit you with my cane like that. You knocked me off balance and I couldn't control where I was waving it."

He frowned in obvious confusion. "Huh?"

I wrinkled my brow in mild concern. "Don't you remember how you ended up on the ground?"

"Uh…" he glanced between me and Chase, his eyes widening when he realized who it was that he'd grabbed onto. "You accidentally hit me with your cane?"

"Exactly. Maybe you should get up now."

He did as I suggested, scrambling to his feet. "Right. Sorry about that."

"No serious harm was done. Next time maybe don't come flying around a corner like that." I patted his arm and then looked at Chase, dismissing the other boy. "Let's go."

Chase's face was still unreadable as he bent down to retrieve my bag, and we continued down the hallway. He didn't take my hand again, but I could sense him looking at me out of the corner of his eye a few times. We drove to my place, and he came into the house with me. I waited until we were both seated at the kitchen table before finally speaking. "Well, that was interesting."

"Why did you lie for me like that?"

I rolled my eyes. "Because I didn't want you to get into trouble."

He frowned. "How did you know that the boy wouldn't argue with you?"

I snorted. "You do know that you have a reputation, right?"

"So?"

"So, that boy was probably so relieved to get out of there without worse injury that he would have agreed to anything. I think I could have told him that a purple elephant knocked him down and he would have agreed just to get away from you."

"Oh." He seemed to consider that for a moment and then his lips curved in the barest hint of a smile. "You're probably right."

I placed my hand over his. "Are you going to explain your reaction to me?"

He grimaced slightly, but nodded. "I don't like to be touched," he mumbled. When I glanced meaningfully at our hands, he shrugged. "You're different."

"How?"

"You know how the other day I said I recognized the same pain in you that I felt? Well, for some reason that made it okay for you to touch me and for me to touch you."

"You don't like touching people?"

He shook his head. "Aside from you, no. If I have enough time to prepare for it, then it isn't always so bad. But if anyone tries to touch me, it usually results in a very negative reaction."

"So all those fights you got into before I met you were because of that?"

"For the most part, yeah. People learned really quickly not to touch me, unless they wanted a fist to their face."

"But it doesn't bother you when I touch you? Or when you touch me?"

He raised his free hand to my face and stroked it lightly. "No. It hasn't from the beginning. That was part of the reason I was so drawn to you."

I thought back over our short acquaintance and realized that there was only one time I'd seen him touch anyone aside from myself. "What about that time you grabbed Adam's wrist in History class?"

Chase's brow furrowed as he thought back, and then his expression cleared. "I'd forgotten about that," he murmured. "Adam was reaching out to grab your shoulder and I reacted instinctively, as if it was me he was trying to touch me instead of you. I'm not entirely sure why that happened."

"So it wasn't something you really planned?"

"No, not really."

"Huh," I replied. "That's strange." I chewed on my lip as I thought about what he'd told me. I wanted to ask him why he didn't like being touched, but I knew he would tell me if he wanted to. With a mental shrug, I gave him a small smile. "We still going out tonight?"

"You still want to go out with me?" he asked, confusion evident on his face.

"Why wouldn't I?"

He frowned. "Because of what I just told you."

"Really? Chase, I have issues of my own. The fact that you don't like people touching you doesn't bug me, since it doesn't seem to apply to me. Why would I change my mind about going out with you?"

"You're not going to ask why I'm this way?"

I cocked my head to one side. "Do you want me to ask?"

He seemed to ponder this for a moment before slowly shaking his head. "No, I don't think I want you to. At least not yet."

I squeezed his hand and then got to my feet. "I'm here if you want to talk. Now, where are we going to go tonight?"

I swung myself onto Justice's back, pleased when my left leg held up without trembling. I squeezed my legs, and Justice moved off into a walk. I let him wander around for five minutes before gathering up my reins a little. "Okay boy, let's try trotting around a little." I nudged him with my legs again and he willingly went into the faster pace.

My body moved with him easily and I automatically started posting to his trot, rising out of the saddle every time his outside shoulder went forward and then sitting as it went back. I could feel the muscles in my bad leg protesting a little, but it wasn't too horrible. I didn't want to push it though, so I only rode him around for another five minutes.

I dismounted and led him over to the arena door. "What did you think?" I asked Chase, who had come down to the barn with me after our date.

He eyed Justice warily as we walked down the barn aisle. "I think you're a little crazy for getting on something that big."

I grinned and led the horse into his stall so I could untack him. "It's not as scary as it may seem," I told him. "Besides, I've been riding since before I could walk. There's a picture of my parents both sitting on horses when Luke and I were only about six months old. My mom was holding me in the saddle in front of her and my dad was holding my brother in front of him. That's how young we were when we started riding."

Chase shuddered slightly. "I can't imagine riding something that huge," he muttered.

I set the saddle down outside the stall and grabbed Chase's hand, pulling him back in with me. I put a brush in his hand and nudged him until he was beside Justice. "Try brushing him. He really likes that."

Chase looked at me in horror and backed up a few steps. "You have got to be kidding me."

"Are you too much of a coward?" I taunted him.

He didn't even blink before responding. "Hell yes."

I sighed and pushed him forward again. "Justice won't do anything to you. I'll stand right beside you the whole time," I promised.

Chase grumbled a little under his breath, but then he cautiously raised the hand holding the brush and ran it down Justice's side. I told him what to do and he slowly relaxed as he brushed the horse rhythmically. "This isn't so bad," he admitted.

"I told you he wasn't that scary." I took the brush from him and put it back in the tack box. Then Chase gathered all the tack for me and we went back into the tack room. We put everything away and then left the warmth of the barn to head back up to the house. When I shivered, Chase put his arm around my waist.

We reached the house and he turned me to face him. He put his warm hand on my cheek and tipped my face up to his. "I had fun tonight. Thanks for not freaking out about what I told you."

"Thanks for watching me ride. That was the first time I tried trotting him."

He pressed his lips to mine in a gentle kiss, and I sighed in pleasure as my free arm slid around him. When he pulled back, his eyes were lit up and he was smiling softly. "I'll call you tomorrow. Maybe we can do something else this weekend."

"I'd like that," I replied, then pulled his head down so I could kiss him again. "Thank you for a wonderful night."

"Anytime." He caressed my cheek once more and then left.

I smiled dreamily and let myself into the house, deciding to grab a drink before going to bed. I went into the kitchen, still lost in my own world, but I stopped dead when I saw that I wasn't alone. I stared at my father, my eyes wide as I tried to figure out why he was still up and if he knew that I'd been down to the barn. He answered my second silent question really quickly.

"Want to explain to me why you were down at the barn so late without telling me or your mother?"

Crap. I was busted.

# Chapter 10

I was silent for a moment as I debated what I should say. Finally, I moved forward and took a seat across from him. "I was visiting Justice."

That obviously wasn't what he'd been expecting me to say, because his eyes widened. "You were?"

"Yeah. I've been going down there every night for almost a month now."

He opened his mouth and then shut it as he digested that. "Oh. Why didn't you tell us?"

I sighed and leaned my elbows on the table. "I was worried that if you knew I was going down to the stables every night you'd think I was all better or something."

"Oh," he said again. "Why did you start going down there?"

I lowered my eyes. "It's hard to explain," I said slowly. "I was in my room one night, and if felt like there was another presence with me. It... pulled me to the stables and then to Justice's stall. It was almost as if Luke was telling me to look after his horse."

My dad was silent for a moment as he obviously tried to collect his thoughts. "Have you had that feeling again?" he finally asked.

"No, but whenever I spend time with Justice, it feels like I'm closer to Luke." I hesitated for a moment before continuing. "I haven't taken a sleeping since the first night I went down to the barn. And I haven't had any nightmares."

My dad sighed and rubbed his hands over his face. "I wish you would talk to us, Dana." He held up a hand before I could reply. "I know it can't be easy for you, but we need to at least know what's going on in your life. I'm not asking you to share your feelings with us or anything, but you need to inform us about things like that. Okay?"

I nodded silently. This was the first time my dad had gotten upset about anything in a while, so I knew I should probably listen to him. "In that case, I should probably let you know that I've started riding Justice."

My dad's jaw dropped and he stared at me for a full ten seconds before speaking. "You're riding him?"

"Yeah, but only walking. Although I did try trotting him a little tonight."

He pinched the bridge of his nose. "I don't suppose there is any point in me telling you it isn't safe to ride alone, is there?"

A tiny smile tugged at my lips. "No, not really. And I wasn't alone tonight. Chase came down there with me."

"So he knew about your nighttime visits?"

I had the grace to look sheepish. "Yeah."

He shook his head. "I don't know whether to be grateful that you can confide in him, or jealous that you'll talk to him."

My shoulders hunched slightly in defense. "Chase is as messed up as I am, dad," I said quietly. "He knows what to ask and when to stay quiet. I never feel any pressure from him to be someone I'm not anymore."

My dad regarded me in silence for a moment. "I think I get it," he replied slowly. "It also probably helps that he never knew Luke, doesn't it?"

That made me stop and think. Was that true? Was part of the reason I was so drawn to Chase because he hadn't known my brother? "I don't know," I started hesitantly. "I never thought about it like that. When I met Chase, I felt something besides emptiness for the first time since the accident. Luke took half of me when he left, and I'll never get that part of me back. But being around Chase somehow makes it more bearable. I don't know how to explain it any better than that."

"You don't have to." He patted my hands and then stood up. "I don't like the idea of you riding alone at night, but I'm not going to try and stop you. Frankly, I'm glad that you're at least going out there, even if it was without us knowing. At least now that I know I can wait up to hear when you come back in at night. That way I'll know you're safe."

I gave him a small grateful smile. "Thanks dad." I got to my feet and surprised him by moving around the table and hugging him. "I'm glad we had this talk. And when I'm ready to share my riding with you, I'll let you know."

His arms wrapped around me as he returned the hug. "I'd appreciate that. Please try and be careful."

"I will be," I promised.

The next day, Chase surprised me by inviting me over to his place. It was the last thing I'd expected him to do, but I was happy to agree. Maybe meeting his foster parents would give me a little insight on him.

He picked me up from my place and drove into town. He pulled into the driveway of a large two story house and parked behind a muscular looking truck. He seemed a little tense as we walked up to the front door, but he didn't say anything until we were about to go in. "I've never brought anyone home before," he mumbled. "I don't know what their reaction will be."

I was suddenly nervous and I took a small step back. "I don't have to come in."

He took my hand and tugged me forward until I was pressed lightly against his side. "I want you to meet them. They'll be nice to you; I think they'll just be shocked at first."

I blew out a breath and nodded my head. "Okay, let's go in."

He opened the door and we went inside. He took my coat from me and hung it up in the front closet before shrugging out of his own and doing the same. Then, taking my hand once more, he led me further into the house. I looked around at everything with interest as we went past a few different rooms. I remembered Chase's comment about how his foster parents had a lot of money, and now I could see what he'd meant.

We reached the kitchen, where a middle aged couple was sitting down playing a game of cards. They glanced up as we came in and both of them did a double take when they saw me. They glanced swiftly at each other and then the woman smiled warmly at me. "Hello."

"This is Dana," Chase said. "Dana, that's Bev and Carson."

I smiled shyly back at them. "Hi."

"It's lovely to meet you," Bev said. "Would you like something to drink?"

I shook my head. "No thank you."

Chase started to pull me out of the room. "We're going downstairs," he said and then led me down the hall to a door. He opened it to reveal a set of stairs that obviously led to the basement. "Can you get down okay?"

I nodded and handed him my cane. I gripped the banister with my right hand and slowly made my way down. Once at the bottom, Chase handed me my cane back. We were in a large open room that was loaded with stuff. There was a large screen TV, a pool table, air hockey table, what looked like a pinball machine and a large assortment of game consoles. "Whoa," I murmured.

"I know, there's a lot of stuff down here," Chase replied. "It was like this when I moved in with them a few months ago. Apparently Carson is just a big kid in disguise."

I smiled as I thought of one of Luke's favorite sayings. "The only difference between boys and men is how much their toys cost," I said.

Chase tilted his head to the side. "I never thought of it like that, but it's true."

"My brother used to say it a lot," I told him, moving to sit down on one of the couches. "So my dad was up when I went in last night."

Chase sat down beside me and raised an eyebrow. "How did that go?"

"Better than I thought it would. We actually had a pretty good talk. I told him about the fact that I was riding Justice, and he wasn't too upset about it. More worried about me riding alone than anything else, I think. But I'm not ready to let anyone to see me ride yet."

"You let me see," he pointed out.

"Yeah, but you're different," I stated.

"How am I different?"

I shrugged. "You just are. I know you won't try and push me into anything."

"Of course I won't." He glanced at the stairs quickly before continuing. "I know what it's like to be pushed into things."

I frowned. "They push you to do stuff?"

He shook his head. "No, not really. These guys are actually pretty decent. But they aren't the only foster parents I've had, and most of the other ones constantly tried to make me 'better'. I hated it. Bev and Carson generally leave me to myself, except for making sure I do my school work and my chores. They don't bug me about not talking. They're actually the first foster parents that I've spoken to since I was put into the system when I was thirteen."

"I thought your parents died when you were ten," I said in confusion.

I sensed him withdraw, though he didn't move. "They did," he said shortly.

Okay, obviously that was a topic he didn't want to discuss. "Sorry," I muttered.

He closed his eyes and sighed. "I didn't mean to snap at you. There are just some things I'm not ready to discuss yet."

"I get it. So, do you want to watch a movie or something?"

He gave me a small smile. "Sure, I'll put something on."

An hour later I was curled up beside him. We had started out on opposite ends of the couch, but somehow we had gravitated towards each other until we were in the middle with his arms wrapped around me and my head on his shoulder. When he turned his head slightly, it was a natural move for me to press my lips to his gently.

The kiss started out the same as all the others, but it quickly became different. He twisted his body and leaned back so that he was lying on the couch, pulling me with him. I ended up between him and the back of the couch, with him facing me. His lips claimed mine again and there was more passion in the kiss than I could ever remember feeling.

I put my left arm around him, since my right one was pinned between us. I ran my hand up and down his back over his t-shirt. Whenever I reached his left shoulder, he would tense slightly, but he didn't say anything so I didn't stop. He slipped one of his hands under the hem of my shirt and traced his fingers over the small of my back, causing me to shiver.

He eventually pulled away and pressed his face into the crook of my neck. We were both breathing a little heavier than usual, but we soon calmed down. When we had settled, he pulled back slightly to look at me. "Can I ask you a personal question?"

"Sure."

"Was Adam your only boyfriend? Or did you date someone before him?"

"No, Adam was the only one. I've known him for a long time and he asked me out when I was sixteen. I said no at first, because I only saw him as a friend, but he eventually wore me down and I said yes. I was with him for just over a year."

"Did you and he ever…" he trailed off, his face turning bright red.

I blushed as well and lowered my eyes. "Yes," I admitted.

"Oh," was his reply.

I peeked up at him form under my lashes. "Does that bother you?"

He was silent for a moment as he thought about it. "No, because you obviously cared a lot for him, and you were together for a long time." He paused and then asked me something that I hadn't been expecting. "Do you think you'd still be with him if the accident hadn't happened?"

The question caught me off guard, and I wasn't sure how to answer it at first. Would I have still been with Adam if it weren't for the accident? "I don't know," I said slowly. "I thought I loved him, and maybe I did. But if our love wasn't strong enough to endure something like that, then maybe it wasn't strong enough to last."

He moved one of his hands up to push a piece of hair out of my eyes. "Aren't teenagers supposed to think that their first love will last forever?"

I smiled sadly. "Maybe normal teenagers," I replied softly. "But you and I aren't exactly normal, are we?"

He kissed the tip of my nose. "I feel normal when I'm with you. Does that count?"

I didn't answer him; I just kissed him again. The movie had been completely forgotten and we spent the next fifteen minutes just wrapped up in each other. When we heard the door at the top of the stairs opened, we pulled apart, but no one came down. "Dana, would you like to stay for dinner?" Bev called down the stairs.

I looked at Chase questioningly and when he nodded I smiled. "That would be great, thank you."

"Okay. It'll be ready in an hour."

When supper was ready, we got off the couch and I made my way over to the stairs. Before I could start up them, Chase moved in front of me and turned his back to me, bending over slightly. "Hop on and I'll carry you up."

"Really?"

"Yeah. You can't be that heavy."

"I'm going to take that as a compliment," I said and then hopped onto his back. I wrapped one arm around his neck and clutched my cane with my other hand. He put his hands on my thighs and started up the stairs.

When we got to the top, he continued to walk instead of stopping like I thought he would. "Aren't you going to put me down?" I asked him.

"Nope," he replied.

I chuckled and rested my chin on his shoulder. "I guess I'll just enjoy the ride then."

He carried me into the kitchen, where Carson was already sitting at the table and Bev was stirring something in a pot on the stove. Carson looked up when we came in and he gave us a crooked smile. "You kids having fun?"

Chase nodded and allowed me to slide down his back onto my own feet again. The meal was really good and I decided that I liked Bev and Carson. Bev was friendly and warm, and Carson was more quiet, but still nice. Chase and I did the dishes and then he showed me his room, which was on the main floor. We listened to music for a little while and then he took me home.

He came down to the barn with me and watched me ride again. Afterwards he helped me brush Justice without any prompting from me. I smiled slightly to myself, thinking that I would turn him into a horse lover eventually.

Once I was in bed later on, I thought back over the past few weeks. I was a little startled to realize that I was actually starting to be happy again. I felt guilty for a moment, wondering if I should really be happy when Luke was gone. But I knew that if he was still here, he'd want me to be happy. So that night, I fell asleep with a smile on my face.

# Chapter 11

"You don't have to come in with me," I told Chase. "You might get bored." It was Tuesday after school, and we were currently sitting outside the building where I did my physical therapy. Chase had offered to drive me there, and now he was saying that he would stay for the session so he could drive me home after.

"I'll be fine, Dana. Come on; let's get in before you're late for your appointment." He got out of the car and waited expectantly for me to join him.

I sighed and climbed out of the car, hunching my shoulders against the biting cold. I went into the building with Chase following along behind me. I put my coat on the hanger in the small waiting area and Chase did the same. We sat down in two of the chairs and waited until it was time for me to go in.

Jared came out of one of the rooms with an older man. "Okay Gerald, I'll see you next week." He turned to me and gave me a warm smile. "Hello Dana. Who's this?" he asked, looking at Chase curiously.

"This is Chase. He volunteered for chauffeur duty today." I got to my feet. "Let's get this over with."

"Chase, would you like to come into the room with us? That is, as long as Dana doesn't mind." Jared glanced at me with a questioning look.

My heart sped up slightly at the thought of letting someone see my leg, but I nodded anyways. "Sure. You'll probably be less bored if you can come in."

The three of us moved into one of the therapy rooms and I hopped onto the padded bench and lay back. I hesitated for a moment before pulling the left leg of my pants up, revealing the mass of scars that covered the entire leg. The leg was also slightly crooked from the crash, but it wasn't nearly as noticeable now as it had been at the beginning.

I couldn't bring myself to look at Chase to see his reaction, so I just closed my eyes and tried to stay still as Jared poked and prodded at my leg. I had to grit my teeth a couple of times to keep from cursing at him, but I managed to stay quiet. He spent twenty minutes massaging the muscles before hooking me up to the machine that he always did. I opened my eyes once he was done that and saw that Chase was sitting in a chair next to my head. Jared wrote a couple of things down on a clipboard and then smiled down at me. "You're doing really well, Dana. Have you been doing the exercises every day?"

I nodded. "Yeah, I do them twice a day. Once when I wake up and once before I go to sleep."

"Good. I think in another month or two you'll be able to get around without the cane."

That perked me up a little. "Really?"

"Yeah. Your left leg will always be weaker than your right, but you should be able to walk without aid again one day."

I heard the front door of the office open, and then a female voice called out. "Jared?"

Jared frowned and stuck his head out the door. "In here Hailey. What's wrong?"

A moment later a young woman appeared in the doorway. "Oh, sorry. I thought you would be done for the day already."

"Dana is my last patient. What are you doing here?"

"I was in the neighborhood and thought I'd stop to invite you over for dinner tonight. Jake and Amanda are coming and I thought you and Cindy would like to join us." She gave him a charming smile. "Actually, I really want Cindy to come; you're just part of the package."

Jared laughed and shook his head. "More wedding plans?"

She nodded. "Yeah, and you know how much Blake starts to whine if I ask him anything about it. According to him we could just get married naked and it wouldn't matter to him since he wouldn't see it anyways." She rolled her eyes .

Jared laughed. "That does sound like something he would say," he replied. Then he seemed to remember where he was. "Crap, sorry. Dana, this is Hailey. I told you about her a little while ago."

I glanced at the young woman in surprise. This was the girl who had been in an accident that tore her life apart? But she was so happy and bubbly. And there didn't appear to be anything wrong with her back. "Hello," I mumbled quietly.

"Hi," she said, smiling warmly. "Have you thought of any colorful names for Jared yet?"

My lips turned up into an answering smile. "Yeah, but I keep them to myself."

"Oh, you should say them out loud. It's very therapeutic to get it out of your system. I had some very creative names that I used to call him when he worked on me." She gave Jared an adoring smile. "And he took it so admirably."

Jared rolled his eyes. "You on your own wasn't so bad. It was when Blake came into it that the names got really colorful."

Hailey chuckled. "That book of insults I bought for him really came in handy for that," she murmured. She glanced over at Chase. "Hi."

I looked at Chase as well and saw that he seemed a little uncomfortable. His eyes met mine and I saw him relax slightly before shifting his gaze to Hailey. "Hey," he muttered.

Hailey glanced between the two of us and a knowing look crossed her face. "Jared, have you shown Chase how to help Dana, like you showed Blake how to help me?"

Jared frowned slightly. "No, this is the first time Chase has been here. And that's not something I usually do, Hales. You and Blake were special."

"I think you should show him, if he's willing. It made a big difference to me." I saw them exchange a look before Jared turned to us again.

"Chase, would you be willing to learn what to do?" He waited until Chase had nodded hesitantly before looking at me. "Would you be willing to let him do that?"

I paled a little at the thought of Chase having to put his hands on my deformed leg. But then Chase placed his hand on my shoulder and squeezed it reassuringly, so I nodded. "Okay."

Hailey chewed on her bottom lip for a moment before speaking again. "Jared, I know this isn't normal protocol, but could you leave the room for few minutes? Chase, you too. I'd like to talk to Dana alone."

Jared was hesitant, but I nodded in agreement so the two of them walked out of the room. Hailey took the seat that Chase had vacated. "It's hard thinking about having Chase touch your leg, isn't it?"

I nodded. "It's not pretty to look at."

Hailey twisted in the chair and raised her shirt up, exposing her back which was covered in scars, much like my leg. She lowered her shirt back down and turned to face me again. "Trust me, I know how you feel."

I was speechless for a moment, absorbing the shock of how her back had looked. "How did that happen?" I whispered.

"Car accident. The back windshield shattered and a bunch of the glass went into my back. Some of the scars are from the glass and some are from all the surgeries I went through." She gestured to my leg. "What happened to you?"

"Car accident as well. My leg got crushed, but they managed to save it." I shrugged my shoulders. "Sometimes I think it would have been better if it had been removed. At least then I'd know exactly what my limitations would be for the rest of my life."

Hailey lifted a brow. "You think losing a leg would limit your life?"

"Yeah."

She shook her head. "It only would have limited you as much as you wanted it to. Blake, the guy I'm marrying, is blind, but it doesn't affect him much. When I met him, he was one of the rudest and nastiest people I knew, because everyone had set limits for him and therefore he'd set them for himself. I helped him realize that being blind didn't make him different, just like the fact that I was occasionally bound to a wheelchair didn't change who I was."

"How did you get better?"

"I pushed myself really hard. If Jared told me to do something, I'd do it twice. It took a lot of work, but I eventually started walking again and now I rarely have to rely on my wheelchair." She sighed and brushed her hair out of her eyes. "At first I wanted to give up, but Jared wouldn't let me. He's my brother's best friend, so I've known him forever. Once he got me out of my stupor, he helped me a lot."

"He said that you lost your parents in the accident."

"Yes, and I nearly lost my brother as well. Did you lose someone in your accident?"

I nodded. "My twin brother."

Compassion filled her eyes and she placed her hand over mine. "That really sucks." She glanced at her watch and swore softly. "I have to go before Blake thinks I got lost." She hesitated briefly. "I'd like to talk to you again, if you don't mind. You remind me of myself, and I'd like to try and help you if I can."

"That would be nice," I replied, surprising myself a little. I hadn't expected to feel so comfortable with someone new so quickly.

Hailey dug into her purse and produced a piece of paper and a pen. She quickly scrawled her number down and then handed the paper to me. "Call me anytime you feel like it. I'm always happy to have new friends, though I can't say the same for the man I'm going to marry," she added wryly. "He's not overly fond of people in general."

I gave her a half smile. "Sounds like Chase. If he doesn't talk to you, don't be offended. He doesn't really talk to anyone aside from me."

She got to her feet and smiled down at me. "It takes a lot to offend me. Next time I talk to you, I'll tell you about the first time I met Blake."

"I'd like that. It was nice to meet you."

"You too. See you later."

She left the room and Jared and Chase came back in a moment later. Jared showed Chase how to massage my leg, and it wasn't as weird as I'd thought it would be having Chase touch my leg. "The more often you can do this, the better," Jared told Chase. "It will help her with the pain."

We left a few minutes later, and Chase turned to look at me before he started the car. "Does your leg hurt you a lot?"

I shrugged. "Not as much as it used to, since it's getting stronger. But there are times when it aches, especially with the weather getting colder. Jared told me I'll always be able to tell when the weather is changing now because of my leg."

"Do you mind me massaging it for you?"

Again I shrugged. "I know it's not pretty to look at, but if you don't mind then neither do I."

"It's part of who you are, Dana. Scars don't bother me." He started the car and pulled out of the parking lot. "Are you hungry?"

The change of subject surprised me, but I nodded. "Yeah, I could eat."

We stopped at a fast food restaurant and had some food and then he drove me back home. "Thanks for driving me today," I said.

"Anytime," he replied, leaning over to give me a light kiss. "I'll see you in the morning."

"Good night." I climbed out of the car and headed into the house. I spent a little time with my parents and then went down to the barn. I no longer had to wait until they went to bed before going down there, since they knew about my visits now.

As I was riding Justice around, Hailey's words about pushing myself came back to me. I urged Justice into a trot and this time I kept it up for a full ten minutes, twice as long as I'd previously managed. My leg was shaking slightly by the time I was done, but I was proud of myself for making it for that long.

Once he was untacked, I spent some extra time grooming him. "We're going to start working harder, boy. I need to get my leg stronger and you need to start working more before you get fat." I ran my hand down his neck. "Plus, I have an idea, but I don't know if it'll work." I gave him a last pat and let myself out of the stall. "Have a good night boy."

# Chapter 12

Winter hit with a vengeance over the next few weeks. The temperature dropped and we got dumped with snow. I was thankful for the heated indoor arena every time I rode Justice. It kept us nice and warm, even when outdoors it was freezing. I continued trotting on him, slowly increasing the amount of time until we were able to do twenty minutes of trot work.

Chase came down to the barn with me a couple of times a week and he slowly grew more comfortable around the horses. I was hoping to get him riding one day soon, but I didn't mention that to him. I knew he wouldn't agree to it yet.

On a cold Saturday morning, Cindy picked me up to take me to the mall so I could do my Christmas shopping. It was the first time we'd gone out of the house together since the accident, and I knew she was really excited about it. And to tell the truth, so was I even though I didn't like shopping. I had missed having girl time with her.

We got to the mall and set out to do our shopping. We spent an hour browsing through the stores before I needed to take a break because of my leg. We went to a small coffee shop and ordered hot chocolates, then settled into a booth. "So how are things going?" Cindy asked me.

I shrugged. "They're getting better," I replied.

"How are things going with Chase?"

I smiled. "Good. He's a really nice guy underneath that tough exterior, and we have a lot in common. I just wish he would trust me enough to tell me more about his past."

"At least he actually talks to you. He's been eating lunch with us for over a month and he still hasn't said a word when Sarah and I are around. I admit that I want to know what his voice sounds like." She blew on her hot chocolate and then took a small sip.

"He doesn't talk to anyone else besides me. He's met my parents a few times now and he hasn't said more than five words to them. And he barely speaks to his foster parents."

"Do you know why he doesn't like talking?"

I shook my head. "No, he hasn't told me. I know that he had a fairly normal childhood until he was ten, but that's it."

"What happened when he was ten?" Cindy asked curiously.

"It's not really my place to tell you," I told her.

"I guess you're right. You can't blame me for being curious though. He's this dark, mysterious person and you're the only one who's gotten close to him. A lot of people are talking about it."

This surprised me. "Seriously? Why?"

"Because you were always popular in school, but now you only hang out with Chase and me. You broke up with Adam and you barely talk to Sarah. People are curious as to why you're interested in a guy who has violent tendencies."

"Violent tendencies? Just because he got into fights at the beginning of the year doesn't mean he has violent tendencies," I defended him.

"I know that, but most people don't really see the two of you together like I do. They judge you two by what they think they see."

I rolled my eyes. "I almost forgot how judgmental people are. I guess most people think I'm a horrible person because I pushed Adam away, don't they?"

"They might have, but Adam won't let them. He's always defended you, no matter what. He holds no resentment towards you and I think he's actually glad that you have Chase to talk to."

I nodded thoughtfully. "He said as much to me when I last talked to him. I'm glad he doesn't hold a grudge against me; he really is a great guy. We just aren't meant to be more than friends now."

"Did you know that he's started seeing someone else?"

"No, I didn't know. Who is it?"

Cindy made a face. "Chantal Bridges."

I wrinkled my nose. "Ugh, he could do so much better than that. What does he see in her?"

"What every guy sees in her. A big chest and very little brains. The ideal woman," Cindy replied dryly. "I don't think he's really serious about her, but he is a teenage boy, and we both know that they aren't always the smartest people around."

"I would try and talk some sense into him if it wouldn't be weird," I said. "But somehow I don't think getting advice from an ex-girlfriend would do any good."

She laughed. "You're probably right. At least she's a fairly nice girl." She took another sip of her hot chocolate. "You know, this is kind of nice."

I knew she wasn't referring to her beverage. "I know. Thanks for not giving up on me."

"You're my best friend, Dana. There was no way in hell I was going to let anything change that."

"I'm glad. So, tell me about your love life."

It was her turn to roll her eyes. "It's non-existent. I haven't found anyone who interests me yet."

"What about that guy from the horse shows last year? I think his name was Kyle."

She shrugged. "Nothing ever came of it. We talked a few times, but I think he was interested in one of the other girls. You know what it's like for guys on the show circuit; the women majorly outnumber them. They can pick whoever they want."

I laughed. "I know. I remember how Luke used to love that. He not only had girls at school after him; he also had girls on the circuit that followed him around like puppies."

Cindy wrinkled her nose. "I remember he used to pretend to be offended that I wasn't falling at his feet like all the others." She stopped suddenly. "Sorry, I know you don't like talking about him."

"It's okay. It's getting easier and easier to talk about him. Besides, I'm the one who brought him up."

We continued chatting for another fifteen minutes and then my cell phone signaled that I had a text. I checked it and saw that it was from Chase. I raised an eyebrow when I read it. "Apparently Chase wants to cook dinner for me tonight. His foster parents went out for the night so he has the house to himself."

"Can he cook?"

"I have no idea. I guess I'll find out tonight." I glanced at the time. "I should probably get going home so I have time to get ready before he picks me up."

"Sure, I'll take you home now."

That evening, I discovered that Chase did know how to cook. He didn't make anything fancy, but the food was good and he'd even dug out some candle and lit them to give the evening a romantic feeling. I helped him do the dishes afterwards and then we went downstairs to watch a movie.

"How was your shopping trip earlier?" he asked as we settled onto the couch.

"It went pretty well. Got most of it done, so I should only have to make one more trip back there. I've never really liked shopping too much, so I'm glad I don't have a lot more to do."

He slid his arm around my waist and tugged me a little closer to him. "That's good. I can take you to do the rest next week if you want."

I laid my head on his shoulder. "Maybe. I don't want to think about it right now; I just want to relax with my boyfriend and watch the movie."

"That sounds like a good idea to me," he replied.

I snuggled into him and let out a contented sigh. His arm tightened around me a little and he kissed the top of my head as the opening credits came on.

Near the end of the movie, I turned my head to kiss him gently. He raised a hand to my cheek and cupped my face. "I didn't think I'd ever be this happy again," he murmured against my lips.

"Me neither," I responded. "Part of me feels guilty, because Luke isn't here and yet I'm starting to be happy again. But I also know that he would want me to live my life and not mourn him forever. It's just hard to pretend that everything is okay when nothing is the same as it used to be."

"Nothing ever stays the same. Change happens daily, though we might not always notice it. Sometimes the changes are really bad, but sometimes they're really good. All the bad things in my life led me to you, so I guess even the bad changes can eventually lead to something good."

"That was sweet," I told him and then brought my lips to his again.

He shifted around so that we were facing each other and pulled his lips away from mine so he could kiss along my jawline. I tilted my head automatically to grant him better access and I felt him smile against my skin. When he nipped at my chin, I yelped and tried to push away from him, but he held me firmly against him. I giggled when he nuzzled at my neck, and he raised his head to look at me, his eyes alight with excitement. "Are you a little ticklish?"

I stopped giggling and stared at him with innocent eyes. "No."

He grinned wickedly. "Oh, I think you're lying to me." His fingers moved to my ribs and he dug them into me lightly.

I squealed and struggled to get away from him, but he just laughed and pinned me down on the couch, tickling me mercilessly. I started laughing so hard that my stomach started to hurt. He looked so happy and carefree at the moment, and that meant more to me than anything else.

Eventually he stopped and gazed down at me with a small smile on his face. "I always have so much fun with you." He released his hold on my hands and framed my face with his long fingers. He touched his lips to mine softly. "I'm so glad that you're in my life."

I put my arms around him and ran my hands up and down his back. "Me too," I replied. He lowered his head to kiss me again, this time for a lot longer. I sighed in pleasure and slid my hands down his back. When I reached the hem of his shirt, I slipped my hands underneath to feel his skin.

A shudder raced through his body, but he didn't break the kiss. Instead, he reciprocated by letting the fingers of his right hand trail down my side to the bottom of my shirt and then going under it to gently trail along my stomach.

I started moving my hands up his back again, but as my fingers reached the bottom of his left shoulder blade, he suddenly froze. I frowned as I encountered uneven skin and moved my fingers up further. The unevenness continued, so I stopped and looked up at him questioningly.

He sat up and moved a little away from me, so I sat up as well. "Chase?"

His eyes were wide and there was a mixture of emotions in them. There was a little anger and some pain, but what surprised me the most was the fear. "I, uh, don't think you should do that," he mumbled.

"Do what? What's wrong?" I reached for him but he shook his head and shuffled back a foot. "Chase, what's going on?"

"Dana, there are things..." he trailed off and his eyes became slightly unfocused for a moment. When they cleared, his expression was blank. "I don't like being touched."

I frowned. "I know, but you've never had a problem with me touching you before." I moved my hands toward him again and ignored the fact that he moved away. I placed them on his upper arms and gave him a small smile. "See?"

He blew out a breath and shut his eyes. "What are you doing to me?"

I pulled my hands back and looked at him in confusion. "What do you mean?"

He opened his eyes to reach forward and grab my hands, bringing them to his lips so he could brush his lips over the knuckles. "I find myself wanting to tell you things that I've never told anyone, not even the shrinks they forced me to see."

"Nothing you say will change how I feel about you. I don't want to push you, but you can trust me with anything. I hope you know that."

"I do know that. It's just difficult for me to drop those last barriers."

I tugged my hands away from his and grabbed the bottom of his t-shirt. I started pulling it up, but he stopped me.

His breathing had become shallow, so I leaned forward and kissed him. He relaxed slowly and allowed me to pull his shirt up. Then he suddenly jumped off the couch. "Let me do this on my own," he said, and then slowly pulled his shirt off over his head. He held it in front of himself for a moment, hiding his body from my view. Then with a shuddering breath, he dropped the shirt.

My eyes widened slightly at the sight of his skin. "Holy crap," I muttered. I struggled to my feet and cautiously placed my hand over his heart. "Chase, what the hell happened to you?"

# Chapter 13

The entire left side of his chest was covered in scars. They extended to the bottom of his ribcage and went up over his shoulder. I took his arm and gently turned him around and saw that the scars continued on his back, though they didn't go as far down as they did on his back. I trailed my fingers over them lightly and he shivered before turning back around to face me. "It's a long story," he said.

"I have all night," I replied. "Can you tell me how this happened?"

He took my hand and sat back down on the couch, tugging me down beside him. "I guess I should start at the beginning. My mom was about eight years younger than my father. She came from a pretty messed up home; her dad was abusive. My dad was a cop and he responded to a domestic violence report at her house. She was eighteen at the time and my dad helped her get out of there and set up on her own. They ended up falling in love and getting married. She cut off all contact with her family, and never saw them again after that day.

"My dad was an only child and his parents had passed away already, so the two of them were on their own until I came along. They wanted more kids, but my mom had some complications and wasn't able to have anymore. So they loved me with everything they had and we were a fairly happy family. I know my mom worried about my dad a lot because of his job, but she was a pretty good cop's wife.

"The day they died was supposed to be the first day of their first vacation together. I already told you that I was staying with a friend of theirs while they were gone. When they died, the courts searched for any living family members that were able to take me. Apparently my mom's father was still alive, but they wouldn't place me with him because of his criminal record.

"Instead, they located my uncle; my mother's older brother. He had a steady job and seemed like a decent guy who was willing to take responsibility for me, so they placed me with him. For the first few months, everything was okay. I had a hard time adjusting to not having my parents any longer, but I was slowly coming around.

"Then one night he came home drunk. I'd never seen him have a drink before, but on this night he was completely plastered. He shoved me around a little and said some things that didn't make much sense to me at the time. The next morning he was back to normal and didn't mention anything about the previous night, so I decided it was a one-time thing."

He paused here and ran his fingers through his hair. "I quickly learned that I was wrong. He started coming home drunk at least once a week and he would push me around and hit me. He'd also tell me that there was nothing I could do about it because I was just a kid and no one would believe me if I said anything. He said that kids who lied got thrown into jail. I was young and still recovering from my parent's deaths, so I believed him. I stopped talking, because everything I said just pissed him off. It continued this way for almost three years before he finally went too far one night.

"He came home drunker than he'd ever been and started his usual routine. Only this time I fought back. That shocked him and he stopped for a few minutes. He started making some coffee, saying he needed to sober up so we could talk like men now that I'd shown some backbone. I don't know why I believed him, but I did. I was feeling pretty proud of myself as I sat at the kitchen table and waited for him to start talking.

"The next thing I knew, he had grabbed the pot of coffee and poured it over my shoulder, screaming at me that I was an ungrateful brat who had ruined his life, just like my father had ruined my mother's by tearing her away from her family. He then grabbed a knife and came at me, so I ran. It was the middle of winter and I was only wearing pajama bottoms and my shoulder felt like it was on fire, but I knew if I didn't run then he would kill me.

"I don't know how long I ran for, but eventually I collapsed on the side of a road and a cop found me. He brought me to the hospital and had me treated. They tried to get me to tell them what had happened, but I wouldn't speak to anyone. They eventually found my uncle the next morning, but he had killed himself, leaving behind a note that stated simply that he was sorry."

He stopped talking and stared at the TV, though I knew he wasn't watching it. I was quiet for a few minutes as I absorbed everything that had happened to him. He'd just been a kid when his parents died and his life had turned to hell. Yet here he was, able to show me compassion and kindness, even if he couldn't show it to anyone else. I laid my head on his scarred shoulder and kissed the side of his neck. "I love you," I murmured.

He jerked slightly and pulled away to look at me. "I tell you all of that and you say that you love me?" he asked incredulously.

I nodded. "You're an amazing person, Chase. The fact that you survived all of that just gives me further proof of that. I knew I loved you before you told me about your past; now just seemed like a good time to let you know."

"Dana, I'm not a good person. I've gotten into a lot of fights in the past, and I probably will in the future."

I rolled my eyes. "I think you should let me judge whether or not you're a good person. The fact that I love you shouldn't be a bad thing; it's supposed to be a good thing."

He took my hand and pressed his lips to the palm of it. "I don't deserve you," he murmured.

"Yes you do," I replied. "Now tell me what happened after you were in the hospital."

He sighed. "I was placed into the system. They shuffled me around from foster home to foster home. I started running to let off steam, since it had saved me in the past. I still refused to talk to anyone unless I absolutely had to and I despised having anyone touch me after what my uncle did.

"Eventually the cop who had rescued me looked me up, and I learned that he had been on the force with my father. He'd been promoted to captain, so he had a little pull in the system. It was only then that I learned the friends of my parents that I'd stayed with had tried to gain custody of me. They weren't registered foster parents at the time though, so they were turned down. The cop pulled some strings and had me placed with them."

My eyes widened. "Bev and Carson were friends with your parents?"

He nodded. "Yeah."

I thought back to the first time I'd hear him speak about them. "But you seemed so bitter about them the first time you said anything about them."

He looked surprised. "I did?"

"Yeah, you were talking about them having money."

He frowned as he thought back and then his expression cleared. "Oh, that had nothing to do with them in particular. It was more the fact that a lot of the foster parents I'd been placed with in the past refused to spend money on a kid like me, since I never stayed with them for long."

"Why don't Bev and Carson adopt you?"

Chase shrugged. "I'll be eighteen next month. There's not much point in them adopting me since I'll be a legal adult on December thirty-first."

"Oh." He hadn't told me about his birthday before, but I let it go for now. "So you get along with Bev and Carson okay?"

"I guess so. Like I said, they leave me to myself for the most part. They know what happened to me and they don't push me into doing or saying anything. And they don't mind that I like to go running a lot."

"Will you stay with them after you turn eighteen?"

"Yeah, at least until I graduate high school. They said I can stay for as long as I want to."

I settled my head on his shoulder again. "Have you thought about what you want to do after high school?"

He hesitated for a moment. "I was thinking of becoming a cop like my dad."

"He'd probably be happy to hear you say that," I said.

"What about you? What do you want to do?" he asked, obviously not wanting to talk about his dad anymore.

"I don't know anymore. Luke and I always planned to go to college for a couple of years before slowly taking over the farm from my parents. But now I'm not sure what I'll do."

"You don't want to run the farm anymore?"

I shrugged. "It wouldn't be the same without Luke with me."

"But would he want you to give up what you'd always planned to do?"

"Probably not," I admitted. "I might just go to college for a year or two to give myself a chance to think about it."

"That sounds like a good idea." He kissed the top of my head. "What do you want to do now?"

I knew that he needed some semblance of normalcy after he'd just revealed so much of his past to me, so I got to my feet. "I know it's cold out, but it's a clear night. Why don't we go sit out on the deck for a little bit?"

He agreed so we went upstairs and grabbed our coats. Once we were bundled into them, we went out to the deck and sat together on the glider. He put his arm around my shoulders and we rocked back and forth slowly. The night was so clear that thousands of stars were visible and I gazed up at them. A feeling of peace settled over me as I sat snuggled against the person I loved.

Suddenly I heard a sound, and I lifted my head to try and hear it better. "Did you hear that?"

"Yeah. What was that?"

I heard the sound again so I got to my feet and hobbled to the stairs of the deck. "It sounds like it's coming from underneath us."

Chase came to stand beside me and he tilted his head when the sound came once more. "I think you're right. Hang on a sec; I'll be right back." He disappeared back into the house and returned a moment later with a flashlight in his hand. "I'll go check it out."

"This is usually the part in movies where a scary monster jumps out and eats you," I muttered as he started down the stairs.

He flashed a grin over his shoulder. "I'm scarier than any monsters out here," he assured me.

I made a face at his back and then leaned against the railing while I waited for him to come back. I heard him moving around under the deck, and a few minutes later he appeared on the stairs again. "I found your monster," he said.

He held out his hands and I saw a small amount of gray and white fluff. When the fluff moved, I realized it was a tiny kitten. "Aw, it's so cute!" I took the little creature from him and cradled it against my chest. "What are you doing out here all by yourself?"

"You do realize that it can't answer you, right?" Chase asked teasingly.

"Just ignore him," I told the kitten. "Come on, let's go inside where it's nice and warm." I cradled it in one arm and went back inside with Chase grumbling behind me.

Once we were back in the warmth, I set the kitten down on the kitchen counter so I could look at it better. It seemed a little skinny, but otherwise it looked okay. It didn't look like it had been away from its mom for too long, and I felt bad for the poor little thing. "Do you have something we can feed it?"

Chase went to one of the cupboards and rummaged through it. "There's a can of salmon," he replied.

"That'll do for now. Can you open the can?"

He sighed in mock exasperation but did as I asked and then set the can on the counter in front of the kitten. The kitten pounced on the food and started scarfing it down as quickly as it could. Chase watched it with amusement. "He's got quite the appetite on him," he stated.

"What makes you so sure it's a boy?" I asked.

"Is it a girl?"

"I haven't checked yet," I replied. "What are we going to do with it?"

"Well, we can't just leave it out in the cold. I'll keep it overnight until Bev and Carson get home and see what they think."

When the kitten finished it's meal, I checked and saw that it was indeed a male. "Okay Starlight, let's get you warmed up now that you're full."

Chase raised a brow. "Starlight?"

I smiled sheepishly. "It seemed like a good name because of all the stars out tonight."

He just chuckled and led the way back downstairs after we'd shed our coats. He had me lay down with my back against the back of the couch. Then he lay down in front of me and settled the kitten on his chest, switching the TV back on with the remote. My eyes grew heavy as I lay curled against his chest and eventually just before i fell asleep, I heard him whisper, "So you know, I love you too."

# Chapter 14

Soft music floated into the room, rousing me from my sleep. I muttered under my breath and snuggled into my pillow more, not quite ready to get up yet. When my pillow moved, my eyes flew open. I blinked a few times in confusion, trying to figure out why I wasn't in my bedroom. When I finally remembered that I had fallen asleep with Chase on the couch, I tilted my head and saw that I was still on his chest and he was sound asleep.

I studied his face for a moment. I'd never seen him quite this relaxed before and it suddenly struck me how handsome he really was. I shifted slightly and pressed my lips against his gently.

He stirred a little and his arms tightened around me as his eyes slowly opened. He blinked at me and then a soft smile crossed his lips. "Good morning."

"Morning," I replied. "I didn't mean to fall asleep on you last night."

"I'm not complaining," he said. "I must admit that I like waking up to you."

I glanced around the room and that's when I noticed that there was a blanket covering us. "How did we end up with a blanket on us? And where's Starlight?"

Chase frowned slightly as he looked around. "I'm not sure." His head tilted to the side. "It sounds like Bev and Carson are home." He glanced at his watch. "Holy crap, it's almost ten. I haven't slept that long in... well, I don't remember ever sleeping this late."

I reluctantly sat up and stretched my arms over my head. Turning to look down at him, I let my eyes roam over his bare upper body and a smile played over my lips. "You know, you're in pretty good shape." I traced my fingers lightly over his abs and my smile widened when he shuddered. "I kind of like it."

His eyes were wary when they met mine. "What about the ugly scars?"

I remembered something he's said to me when he'd come to my physical therapy with me for the first time. "Scars don't bother me." I bent my head and kissed his marred shoulder. "They give you a dangerous quality."

He snorted. "Yeah, because having coffee poured over me makes me really dangerous," he said dryly.

I trailed my lips along the line of scars. "I think they're kind of sexy."

He grasped my chin and pulled my mouth up to his for a long kiss. "I think you're kind of sexy," he murmured against my lips.

It was my turn to shiver and I pulled away from him. "I think we should go upstairs and find Starlight," I said in a slightly breathless voice.

A grin stretched across his face as he sat up. "I embarrassed you, didn't I?"

"Maybe," I mumbled, knowing that my face was slightly red.

He chuckled and kissed my cheek. "You're kind of cute when you blush."

I rolled my eyes and got to my feet. "Come on, let's go up."

He gave me a piggy back ride up the stairs and then set me down. We went into the kitchen and found Bev at the stove flipping pancakes while music flowed out of a small radio. She turned when we came in and smiled at us. "Good morning."

"Morning," Chase muttered. "Where's the cat?"

Her eyes lit up. "Oh, you mean that adorable little ball of fur? Carson has him in the den. Where did you find him?"

"Under the deck last night," I replied. "We couldn't just leave him out there."

"Goodness, of course you couldn't. Will you be taking him home?" she asked.

I hesitated. "I was hoping he could stay here, actually. All our cats stay down at the barn and I think he's too little to be down there."

Relief flashed across her face. "Oh good, because I already went out and bought some stuff for him this morning. Does he have a name yet?"

"Starlight, since there were so many stars out last night." I took a seat at the table and Chase sat next to me.

"That's a good name for him." She flipped another pancake. "Your breakfast will be ready shortly."

I leaned my elbows on the table and dropped my chin onto my hands. "Did you put the blanket on us last night?"

"Actually, Carson did that. He went down to watch some TV and found you guys down there. I hope you don't mind Dana, but I called your parents and let them know where you were."

My eyes widened and I straightened in my seat. "I didn't even think about that. Thanks for calling them. They would have been really worried otherwise."

"You're welcome dear," she said, setting a plate of pancakes in front of each of us. "Enjoy."

Chase and I ate our breakfast in silence and then I called my parents. They weren't upset about me being out overnight, which surprised me a little. But then I realized that they were probably just happy that I was socializing so much again. I let them know that I'd be home later and then hung up the phone. "Well, I think they've decided they like you," I informed Chase.

He raised an eyebrow. "What makes you say that?"

"They didn't freak out about the fact that I stayed the night with you," I replied. "If they didn't like you, I would've gotten yelled at."

"Huh." He looked down at his hands. "I didn't think they'd approve of me. I'm not exactly a parents ideal choice for their daughter."

"You're the perfect choice for me, and they know that. They've seen how much I've improved since I met you."

He placed a hand over mine. "Bev and Carson really like you to, and I have a feeling it's for the same reason. I actually had a full conversation with Carson the other day."

"Really? About what?" I asked curiously.

His cheeks turned a little red and he turned away from me. "I didn't know what to get you for Christmas," he mumbled. "So I asked Carson for some ideas."

"What did you decide on?"

His eyes flicked back over to me and a smile tugged at his lips. "I'm not telling you."

I pouted a little. "Meanie."

"What did you get me?" he challenged.

"Not telling," I responded, sticking my tongue out at him.

He laughed and shook his head. "That was really mature."

I grinned. "I know." I glanced at the clock. "So, what do you want to do today?"

I was in a great mood on Monday when I got to school. I'd spent the rest of the day yesterday just hanging out with Chase and his foster parents, mainly playing with Starlight who was already being spoiled rotten. The morning went by like it normally did, but when lunch came around, I found Chase waiting for me outside the cafeteria with a scowl on his face. "I hope that look isn't for me," I said.

His expression lightened slightly when he saw me. "No, it's not for you."

I was surprised that he'd actually answered me, since there were people around. I took his hand and led him to an empty stairwell. "What's wrong?"

He sighed and leaned back against the wall. "I got paired with someone for a project last period," he muttered.

I frowned. "But they don't usually do that." The teachers in the school usually allowed Chase to do projects on his own, since he wouldn't speak to anyone. "Why did you get paired with someone?"

"There were an uneven number of students in this class, and the project has to be done in pairs. It can't be done alone or in groups of three."

"That sucks. What are you going to do?"

He ran his hands over his face in a gesture of frustration. "I don't know. How the hell am I supposed to do a project with someone when I won't talk to them?"

I chewed on my lower lip as I thought about it. "Are you supposed to work on it outside of school?" When he nodded, I moved a little closer to him. "Would it help if I was there whenever you had to do that? It won't help during your class, but it might make it easier for you at home."

He visibly relaxed his posture and put his arms around me. "That would definitely help." He brushed his lips over my temple. "I'll make sure any after school work is done at my place. It doesn't start until after the holidays, so at least I don't have to worry about it until then."

"Now that we've got that settled, can we go eat? I'm kind of hungry."

He grinned and nodded, pushing us away from the wall and heading back to the cafeteria. "You're a pretty awesome girlfriend," he stated as we walked.

"You're not too bad as a boyfriend, either," I replied. "Who'd you get paired with for the project?"

"A girl named Vicky Morgan."

I stopped dead and turned towards him. "Please tell me you're joking."

"I wish I could, but I'm not. Why?"

I grimaced. "Vicky and I have never really gotten along that well. She had a thing for Luke and he didn't reciprocate. For some reason, she always blamed me and has been nasty to me ever since."

Chase groaned. "Something tells me that this after school work is going to be very interesting."

"Oh yeah. It'll be a laugh a minute," I replied dryly. "Let's go eat."

# Chapter 15

I slid my right leg back behind the girth and squeezed. Justice immediately leaped into a canter and I couldn't keep the smile from breaking out across my face. This was my first day trying the faster gait, and the familiar rocking motion was strangely comforting. I kept it up for three circuits of the arena and then slowed him down, the grin still plastered on my face. I brought Justice to a halt near Chase. "What did you think?"

"I think you're crazy for wanting to go that fast on a horse," he remarked wryly. "But you also looked like you were having a lot of fun up there."

"It's an amazing feeling," I gushed, sliding off of Justice. I removed my helmet, shaking my hair out of my eyes. "I think we'll be ready to start jumping soon."

He shuddered. "I don't know if I'll be able to watch you do that."

I slid a glance over to him as we walked down the barn aisle towards Justice's stall. "Aw, do you worry about me?"

"Of course I do. I love you."

My heart stuttered and I leaned into him when he put his arm around my waist. "I love you too." We untacked Justice in companionable silence. When we were finished, we left the stables to go up to the house. "Jesus, it's freezing out here!" I wrapped my coat tighter around me, trying to block out the bitter wind.

"I think it dropped about ten degrees while we were in there," Chase said in agreement.

"It's times like this that I wish I could still run. At least- ack!" my musings were cut off when Chase scooped me into his arms and sprinted the rest of the distance up to the house. I was laughing by the time we got to the door and he put me back on my feet. "Well, that's one way to get out of the cold quicker," I told him.

He grinned down at me while I opened the door. "I didn't want to stay out there any longer and I wasn't exactly going to leave you out there to fend for yourself."

I wrinkled my nose at him. "You can be so cute sometimes."

He rolled his eyes and moved into the kitchen to make us some hot chocolate. "Where are your parents?"

"Out for the night," I replied. "They went to the Christmas party that one of the boarders here throws every year."

"You didn't want to go?" he asked.

I shook my head. "No. I'm not ready for stuff like that yet."

He nodded and continued making the hot chocolate. I loved that he understood me so well. I never had to explain my feelings to him, which made it so much easier to be around him. When the drinks were ready, we brought them into the living room so we could watch a movie while we drank them. I let Chase choose the movie, but instantly regretted it when I realized he'd chosen a scary one. "I hate horror movies," I whined.

He smiled wickedly. "I know, but I love your reactions to them," he replied.

I rolled my eyes and put my head on his shoulder, clutching his left arm with both my hands. He chuckled and reached across with his free hand to rest it on my knee.

By the time the movie was fifteen minutes in, I was no longer sitting beside him. Instead, I was curled into a ball on his lap with a death grip on his neck and my face pressed into his throat. He hadn't stopped laughing since the first time I'd screamed, so now I retaliated by nipping at his skin. He yelped and pulled back, glaring down at me. "What was that for?"

"For being so mean," I retorted. "It's not nice to laugh at your girlfriend so much."

"Oh come on. You have to admit that your reactions are pretty funny."

I sniffed and turned my face away. "I admit nothing." Unfortunately, I was now facing the TV again and I saw someone get brutally murdered. I let out a squeak and buried my face in his chest. "Can we please watch something else?"

"No way, this movie is awesome."

I groaned and snuggled into him more, wriggling around to try and get more comfortable. I froze when he suddenly tensed. I looked at his face and saw that his expression was suddenly strained. "Chase? What's wrong?"

He cleared his throat. "Uh, maybe you, um, shouldn't move around quite so much." His cheeks were tinged with pink and he refused to meet my eyes.

It only took me a moment to realize the problem, and then my cheeks heated slightly as well. "Oh." I hesitated for a moment before talking again. "Chase, do you want... more from this relationship? Physically, I mean."

"I don't want anything that you aren't ready for," he replied.

"And what if I wanted more?" I whispered.

He raised his eyes to mine, and I saw that they were now bright with excitement. "I'm a guy, Dana. I'm up for pretty much whatever you want to do."

I chewed my lower lip for a moment as I thought about it. Then I reached for the remote and turned the TV off. I cut off his protests with a long kiss. "I think you should take me to bed now," I told him.

He didn't hesitate to do as I requested.

The next morning I was eating breakfast with my parents when an idea came to me. "Do you think we could invite Chase and his foster parents over here for Christmas dinner? I know it's short notice, but Chase mentioned the other day that they didn't have any big plans."

My parents exchanged glances. "Sure, you can invite them. Maybe we can even hook Autumn up and go for a sleigh ride," my dad suggested.

"That would be fun!" Autumn was one of our lesson horses, but he was also broke to drive. "I'm going to go give Chase a call now and see if they can come."

Chase asked his foster parents and they were happy to agree. Bev asked if there was anything she could bring, so I told Chase to have her call my mom and find out. Then we arranged to go out for dinner together that night before we hung up the phone.

I spent the day hanging around the house, reading a new book that Cindy had leant to me. I was so engrossed in it that I didn't even hear Chase knock on the door, so when he came into view I jumped slightly. He chuckled and sat on the couch beside me. "Good book?" he asked.

"Yeah, Cindy got me hooked on them. They're pretty good."

"Are you ready to head out? Or would you rather just keep reading this amazing book?" he teased.

I grinned at him. "You're in a pretty good mood," I observed.

"After last night, I'm an awesome mood," he stated.

I rolled my eyes. "Such a guy," I mumbled, and grudgingly set my book down. "Come on, let's get out of here. I didn't realize how hungry I was until now."

We had a great time out together and he came to the stables to watch me ride Justice after. When I was done riding, I dismounted and then tilted my head slightly, regarding Chase thoughtfully. When he saw me looking at him, he raised an eyebrow. "What?"

I took my helmet off and held it out to him. "It's time for you to learn to ride. I'll lead you around."

He shook his head. "No way. I am not getting up on that thing."

"Aw, come on. Please?"

He hesitated for a moment, but then shook his head again. "No."

I sidled a little closer to him and slid the arm that wasn't holding Justice's reins around his neck. "Please? I really want you to try." I nuzzled his neck lightly. "It would mean a lot to me."

He blew out a breath that wasn't quite steady. "Damn it. I'm never going to be able to say no to you again, am I?"

I gave him an innocent smile. "I have no idea what you're talking about."

He snorted. "Yeah right." He sighed and took a step back. "Give me the damn helmet."

I grinned and passed it over to him, helping him buckle it on. "You look so cute!" I gushed.

He glared at me. "Shut up. How the hell do I get on this thing?"

I led Justice over to the mounting block and told Chase to climb onto it. "Now put your left foot in the stirrup and swing your right leg up and over his back. Just try not to kick him in the butt when you do it."

Chase grumbled under his breath, but did as I said and cautiously swung onto Justice's back. He gripped the horse's mane tightly with both hands while I went to his right side to help him get his foot in that stirrup. Then I looked up at him. "Ready?"

"No, but somehow I don't think that's going to stop you from making him move anyways."

I laughed and moved ahead a few steps. Justice followed me obediently, while Chase's knuckles went white from how tight he was hanging on. Then I grabbed my cane from where it was leaning against the wall and started leading them around the arena. I glanced back every minute or so to check on Chase, and I saw his grip loosen slightly as we went along. We made two full circuits before I stopped. "There, that wasn't so bad, was it?"

He pretended to glare at me for a moment, but then his lips turned up into a reluctant smile. "No, it wasn't too horrible."

I told him how to dismount, and then we worked together as usual to put Justice away for the night. When we were walking back up to the house again, I tucked my arm through his. "Thank you."

"For what?"

"For trying that."

He shrugged. "It wasn't as scary as I thought it was going to be. I may even let you get me on a horse again."

"Really? That would be great! I'd love to be able to go on a trail ride with you once the weather gets nicer again."

He looked down at me when we stopped at the door. "I didn't know it would mean that much to you."

It was my turn to shrug. "Luke and I used to go trail riding together all the time. I'd like to be able to do something with you that I always enjoyed doing with him."

He wrapped his arms around me and hugged me tightly. "In that case, you can start teaching me every night that I'm here, if you want to."

I kissed him on the lips gently. "You really are an amazing guy, you know."

He grimaced. "Only to you," he mumbled.

I shook my head. "No, not only to me. You just don't show this side to anyone else yet, but you will one day. Look at how much you love Starlight already."

"He's a kitten. It's kind of hard to hate something that cute."

I chuckled and kissed him once more before pulling reluctantly away. "I'll see you tomorrow."

He ran the back of his hand down my cheek. "Have a good night."

"You too. I love you."

"Love you too, Dana. Sleep tight."

# Chapter 16

On Christmas Eve, I stood in the doorway of the kitchen, gazing at my parents uncertainly. They were both engrossed in a card game and they hadn't noticed my arrival yet. I cleared my throat, and they both turned to look at me. "I was wondering if you guys wanted to come watch me ride Justice tonight."

They were speechless for a few moments as they absorbed what I had said. Then they both got to their feet quickly, the card game forgotten. "Of course, if you're sure you want us to," my mom said.

"I'm sure. I want to try jumping him tonight, and I want you both to be there." I turned and walked away before they could say anything else. I wasn't sure if I'd be able to deal with it if either of them got emotional on me now.

We walked down to the barn together, with me picking my way carefully around the ice. When we reached the stables, I went to Justice's stall immediately. Like every night, he stuck his head over the door and nuzzled me. "Hey boy. I hope you're ready for this tonight."

My dad moved off to the tack room while I brushed Justice. When my dad returned, he was laden down with tack, which my mom quickly helped him set down. He'd also grabbed my helmet for me, and I smiled at him in thanks. I got Justice ready, and I was pleased that my parents didn't offer to do it all for me. I didn't mind if Chase helped me, but that was mainly because I was teaching him what to do, rather than needing his help.

I led Justice out of the stall, my cane making its usual rhythmic tapping sound as we went down the aisle. Once in the arena, I put my helmet on, placed my cane against the wall and then maneuvered Justice by the mounting block. I climbed on and got myself settled, then squeezed with my legs to move him forward.

My parents stayed silent the whole time I warmed him up, but I could tell by the looks on their faces that they were incredibly happy that I'd allowed them to watch this. When Justice was sufficiently warmed up, I looked at my dad. "Think he's ready for me to take him over a small jump?"

He nodded and walked over to where two standards were set up with a bunch of poles lying beside them. He set up a low cross rail and then stepped back. "Okay, take him over it."

I urged Justice to a trot, trying to ignore the butterflies in my stomach. I knew this was the true test of my new bond with this horse. My parents had said that he wouldn't even jump tiny jumps like this without knocking them down. I kept my eyes up as we approached the small obstacle. Justice didn't even hesitate as he deftly leapt over it, easily clearing it and landing in a canter. I grinned as I brought him back to a trot and took him around and over it again. When he cleared it effortlessly once more, I gave him a pat. "Good boy," I crooned to him.

I slowed him to a walk and approached my parents again. My dad smiled up at me. "Well, he obviously still knows what to do, at least with you up there. Are you going to keep jumping him?"

I was quiet for a moment as I thought of the plan I'd come up with a couple of weeks ago. I wasn't sure what my parents would think of it, but I decided to tell them anyways. "I want to enter him in the first show of the season."

Both of them froze in place. My mom opened and closed her mouth a few times before finally speaking. "Y-you want to go to that show?"

I nodded and looked down at my hands. "I want to ride in Luke's memory," I whispered. "I think that's what he would want me to do."

My dad stepped forward and laid one of his hands over mine. "I think you're right." He looked over at my mom. "What do you think?"

"I think as long as her physical therapist clears it, then it shouldn't be a problem." She moved up to stand beside my dad, and placed her hand over both of ours. "Thank you for letting us watch you. It's the best Christmas present I could've asked for."

I didn't say anything else after that, and I got off Justice and put him away. We all went back up to the house and my dad lit the fireplace in the living room. My mom made us some hot chocolate and we sat around the fire, all of us lost in our own thoughts. It felt weird sitting around the fire on Christmas

Eve without Luke there. We'd done this every year for as long as I could remember, and it felt empty without him.

After half an hour, I couldn't handle it anymore and I went to bed. I called Chase and talking to him made me feel a little bit better. When I hung up, I settled down into my pillows. Sleep eluded me for nearly two hours, but eventually I drifted off, only to wake up an hour later with my heart pounding and my breathing rapid. I'd had a nightmare, but I didn't remember what it was about.

I got out of bed and went to the kitchen to get myself a drink of water. Then I went into the living room and curled up on the couch. For some reason, I didn't want to go back into my room tonight. I tried to fall asleep on the couch, but I didn't have any luck. I was dead tired when my parents eventually woke up in the morning and came down, but I tried to hide it from them. I don't think I did a very good job of it, but they didn't comment on it as we opened presents before they went to the barn to do chores.

I sent Chase a text, asking if he could come over earlier than his foster parents. He replied back right away saying that he could come over now, and I was more than happy to agree. He showed up twenty minutes later, took one look at me, and dragged me into my room. I was a little startled, but then I smiled slightly. "You do know that my parents will be back in the house shortly, right?"

He rolled his eyes. "You look like hell, Dana. I didn't bring you in here for that."

Hurt flashed through me and I yanked my arm away from him. "Gee, thanks," I said sarcastically. "If you're just going to insult me, maybe you should leave."

He looked surprised, but then his eyes softened a bit. "Sorry, that came out wrong. You just look really tired and I want you to have a nap."

I lowered my eyes. "Oh. I didn't really get to sleep last night."

He cupped my cheek in his hand. "What happened?"

I sighed and sat down on the bed, then explained everything that had happened. "I think there were just too many things running through my mind. And the nightmare made me afraid to go back to sleep."

Chase stretched out on the bed and held his arms open. "Lay with me and try and get some sleep now," he said. "I'll stay with you."

I didn't have to be told twice. I laid on my side and put my head on his chest, curling my left arm around his waist. His arms came around me and held me snugly against him. I listened to the steady rhythm of his heartbeat, and it soothed me. My eyes grew heavy, and sleep finally overcame me.

I woke up when someone knocked on my bedroom door softly. I pried my eyes open and realized I was still curled up against Chase. His eyes were open and he was looking down at me with a small smile on his face. "Good morning," he murmured.

I stretched and glanced at the clock beside my bed, doing a double take when I saw that it was almost two in the afternoon. "I don't think it's morning anymore."

He chuckled. "No, I guess it's not. Are you feeling better?"

I nodded and sat up. "A lot. Thanks."

He sat up as well and rubbed my back. "Anytime. We should probably get up. Your mom said that she would knock on the door when it was time almost time for Bev and Carson to get here."

I had started to get out of bed, but now I stopped and looked at him. "When did she say that?"

"About an hour after you fell asleep, she came in here looking for you. When she saw that you were sound asleep, she told me she'd knock to let us know when we should get up."

I shook my head in amazement. "She never would have been okay if Adam had been in my room alone with me like that."

"Things are different now," he said simply.

"They definitely are." I got off the bed and walked over to my dresser. I grabbed the envelope that was sitting there and handed it to Chase. "Merry Christmas."

He stood up and reached into his pocket, pulling out a small wrapped box. "Merry Christmas." He handed the box to me and then sat back on the bed to open the envelope.

I sat beside him and pulled the wrapping paper off the package. A small jewelry box was revealed, and I studied it curiously for a moment before opening it. A small gold heart shaped locket was nestled inside, and I smiled as I pulled it out. I opened it, and my smile faded as I gazed at the pictures inside.

On one side there was a picture of Justice that I recognized as one that had been taken a couple of years ago. On the other side, there was a miniature picture of Luke with his trademark smile in place. I stared at the picture, remembering the day it had been taken. It had been our seventeenth birthday party, and we'd had a great day. It seemed like such a long time ago now, even though it was just over a year ago.

Gentle fingers suddenly grasped my chin, and I turned to look into Chase's concerned green eyes. "Do you not like it?" he asked worriedly.

I threw my arms around his neck, nearly toppling him over backwards. "I love it," I told him. "But where did you get the pictures?"

"From your parents."

I stared at him in shock. "You actually talked to them?"

A wry smile touched his lips. "Yeah, and I don't know who was more shocked. Me or them."

I touched my lips to his in a long, gentle kiss. "Thank you. This means a lot to me."

He blew out a relieved breath. "Good. I wasn't entirely sure what your reaction would be." He held up the two tickets that I had bought for him. "How did you manage to get these? They've been sold out for over a month."

I smiled. "That's for me to know. All you need to know is that you'd better use the second ticket for me."

He laughed and hugged me tightly. "Who else would I use it for?"

"Good point. Now let's get up and go for a sleigh ride."

The rest of the day went by quickly. I ended up having a good time with everyone, and I think my parents were relieved to see me get out of the funk I'd been in that morning. We all went for a sleigh ride, and my parents had even put bells on Autumn's harness, so it jingled merrily as we trotted along.

When Chase and his foster parents had left for the evening, my parents and I once again sat around the fireplace together. I rubbed my left leg absently as I looked into the dancing flames. "You guys seem to like Chase a lot," I said, breaking the silence.

"We do," my dad replied. "He's been really good for you over the past couple of months."

"Is that why you didn't freak out when we fell asleep at his place the one night? And why you were okay with us being in my room earlier today?"

"You're eighteen now, Dana. And you're a lot more mature than most people your age. You've gone through something that no one should ever have to go through, and you're dealing with it remarkably well now. Chase is part of the reason you're able to do that. We trust you to be responsible with him and that you won't do anything you aren't ready for."

I nodded and continued looking into the fire. "Thanks," I finally mumbled. "I know it hasn't been easy for you guys either since Luke died. It was hard on all of us, but I just couldn't deal with anything at first. You're right when you say Chase has helped me a lot. I don't know what I would've done without him." I got to my feet, trying not to wince at the twinge of pain in my leg. "I love you both. Good night."

They both murmured their own goodnights to me, obviously a little surprised at my words. I went into my bedroom and got ready for bed. I was pretty tired still, so I didn't think I'd have any problem falling asleep. Sure enough, as soon as my head hit the pillow, I was out like a light.

But like last night, I didn't sleep long. Only it wasn't a nightmare that woke me up tonight. Excruciating pain tore through my left leg, and a scream ripped its way out of my throat. I heard a thud from upstairs and then the sound of feet running, but before my parents could reach me, everything went black.

# Chapter 17

Darkness.

Complete and total darkness. That was the first thing I became aware of when my mind slowly started to function once more. It took me a few minutes to realize that it was only dark because I had my eyes closed. Once I was aware of that, I forced my lids to open. A strange feeling of déjà vu surrounded me as I realized I was in a hospital room. I once again had an IV in my arm, but I wasn't surrounded by machines this time.

I tilted my head to the side and saw my parents talking quietly to a doctor in the doorway of the room. I shifted in the bed slightly and noticed that my left leg felt a little heavier than it had before, but the horrible pain was gone. It was still sore, but it was bearable now. My movement caught the attention of the three people in the doorway, and they hurried over to me.

"How arc you feeling?" my mom asked.

"A little groggy," I replied. "What happened?"

The doctor stepped forward, and I recognized him. It was Dr. Green, the same doctor I'd woken up to all those months ago. He smiled down at me. "Hello Dana. You had a blood clot in your leg, which is what caused the pain. Normally it wouldn't have hurt so much, but since the leg is so damaged already, it affected it a lot more. We did a minor surgery to remove it and we also placed an IVC in the vein to prevent that from happening again."

"How did I get a blood clot?"

"It happens sometimes after surgery or trauma. Normally it happens a lot sooner after these events, but it's not unheard of for it to take this long. Did you feel any pain before you went to bed?"

"A little, but it wasn't that bad. Will I have to use my crutches again?"

"Maybe for the first couple of weeks, but then you should be able to go back to your cane. We're going to keep you in here for a few days for observation and to give you a few injections. We'll also give you a prescription of blood thinners for you to take once you're released. You'll have to come in for regular blood tests for a while though."

I grimaced. "Ugh, I hate needles.

He patted my right foot. "I don't blame you. But hopefully we can prevent this from happening again. You need to take it easy for a little while."

I hesitated for a moment. "I've started riding again. How long will it be before I can do that again?"

He thought about it for a moment. "I'd say a month to be safe. You might be able to get away with three weeks if your physical therapist says it's okay. We'll just have to play it by ear."

I sighed. "Okay. Thanks Dr. Green."

"Anytime. I'll leave you with your parents now. I'll be back to check on you in a few hours." He left the room after making a couple of notes on my clipboard.

I turned to my parents. "Sorry if I scared you guys."

My dad sat down heavily in the chair beside my bed. "Scared is putting it mildly. I nearly fell down the stairs in my hurry to get to you." He put his hand over mine. "Why didn't you tell us your leg was hurting you earlier?"

"It really wasn't that bad. I didn't think anything was wrong with it."

He rubbed his hands over his face. "Well, I think I may have lost five years of my life, but I'm glad you're okay."

I gave him a sheepish smile. "Sorry," I murmured. "What time is it?"

"Almost nine in the morning. We called Chase about twenty minutes ago, so I-"

His voice was cut off when we heard a minor commotion outside my room. A few seconds later, Chase came into the room, ignoring the nurse who was telling him it was only family allowed in the room. He moved quickly to the side of the bed and grabbed my hand. His eyes met mine, and I saw a wide range of emotion pass over his face before it settled on relief. He didn't say anything as he looked down at me, but he didn't need to. I knew exactly what he was feeling.

I heard my dad murmuring something to the nurse, and then he and my mom left the room, leaving me alone with Chase. I scooted over in the bed slightly and he immediately sat down and carefully put his arm around me. Then he put his cheek on top of my head and blew out a long breath. "You okay?"

I shrugged. "I will be. They're making me stay in here for a few days."

"Why?"

I told him what the doctor had said, and Chase nodded before falling silent once more. We cuddled together on the narrow bed, neither of us saying anything. I took comfort in his arms, somehow feeling like this would all be okay as long as he was with me.

After a few minutes of silence he kissed my temple. "I was scared when your dad said you were in the hospital," he murmured.

"I think I scared a lot of people tonight," I replied. "I'm sorry for that."

"It wasn't your fault." He held me a little tighter. "I just don't know what I would do if something happened to you."

"Well, you don't have to worry about that now. The only thing you might have to worry about is me going completely nuts while I'm in here."

"I'll keep you sane," he promised.

"How do you plan on doing that?"

"I dunno. But I'll figure something out." He nuzzled my hair. "Do you need anything right now?"

"No, just don't leave me."

"I won't."

Two days later, I was going stir crazy. They refused to let me leave, and I was becoming cranky and snappy. I'd gotten so used to freedom that being confined drove me nuts. Chase was a rock for me, never letting my attitude deter him from staying with me. When he came in to see me that morning, he was glancing around surreptitiously. When he saw that I was alone, he carefully undid his coat. A pair of tiny eyes peered out at me, and I felt my face split into a grin. "Starlight," I crooned, reaching for him.

Chase placed him in my arms. "If I could've snuck Justice in here, I would've. But somehow I don't think I could have fit him under my coat."

I laughed. "No, I don't think that would've worked. I can't believe you smuggled a kitten into here."

"I knew he would make you smile," he said. "I know it isn't easy for you to be stuck in here."

I made a face. "No, it's definitely not."

"How was your night?"

"It wasn't too bad. They let me get up and walk around this morning, and my leg didn't hurt so badly afterwards."

"That's good. Have they told you when they'll be letting you leave here?"

I sighed. "Not for another two days at the earliest. They want to make sure I don't have a reaction to the injections before they let me leave."

"Too bad this didn't happen two weeks from now. At least then you could've been missing school, instead of having to spend your school vacation in here."

"You're spending it here, too. You don't have to stay here with me the whole time, you know. I'd understand if you wanted to go do other stuff. I'd be mad at you, but I'd understand."

He rolled his eyes. "Where else would I want to be?"

I shrugged. "I dunno. I do feel a little bad about you being stuck here with me, though."

He sat down on the edge of my bed. "I'm not going to leave you alone, Dana. What kind of boyfriend would I be if I did that?"

"A pretty sucky one," I admitted. "I called Hailey earlier and asked her if she'd come by. She told me that if I ever need to talk to someone, I could call her. I know she's had some relapses with her back, so I'm hoping she'll be able to help me through this."

"That's the girl from the physical therapy place, right?"

"Yeah, Jared's friend. I really liked her and I want to talk to her again. Did you know that here fiancé is blind?"

He raised an eyebrow. "No, I didn't. That's got to be a little weird."

"I know. I wonder how they met."

"If she said she would come visit you, then you can ask her. I'm going to sneak Starlight out of here before they catch me. I'll be back shortly." He gave me a light kiss, stuck the kitten back under his coat, and then left the room.

A couple of hours later, we were playing a game of cards. My parents had already been by to see me, but I'd encouraged them to go back home since Chase was there and Hailey would be visiting me later on. Cindy had said she would stop by later on as well, so I knew I wouldn't be bored.

"Do you have any three's?" I asked Chase.

He narrowed his eyes at me. "I don't know how, but you're cheating," he stated as he handed over a card.

I grinned at him. "I've never met anyone who actually sucks at this game. It's kind of funny."

There was a knock on the door, and I glanced over to see Hailey standing in the doorway, holding the hand of a blond guy. The guy was wearing sunglasses, and it only took me a second to realize that this must be her fiancé. "Hey Hailey."

"Hey Dana. How are you doing?"

"I've been better," I replied. "Come on in."

She tilted her head up and murmured something to the guy beside her, and then she came forward, easily steering him around any objects. "Dana, Chase, this is Blake, my fiancé. Blake, this is Dana, the girl I told you about, and her boyfriend Chase."

"Nice to meet you," I said.

Blake nodded to us, and then scowled when Hailey elbowed him in the ribs. "What?"

She rolled her eyes. "We've been over this before. Stop being an ass and say hi to them."

He made a face at her, but then smiled slightly. "Hi." He turned his head back to Hailey. "Happy now?"

"Ecstatic," she replied sarcastically before looking at me. "Told you he's not good around people."

I chuckled. "It's okay." I glanced at Chase. "He's kind of the same way."

"I'm not that bad," Chase protested. "I just don't like talking around other people."

My brows rose in mild surprise. "You're talking around them," I pointed out.

He opened his mouth to reply, then shut it and frowned thoughtfully. "Huh, that's weird," he mused.

"I have that effect on people," Hailey said cheerfully. "Blake was a complete jerk when I met him, but now he's... well, he's still a jerk, but at least he's not as rude anymore."

"Sitting right here, Hales," Blake said dryly.

"So? You were a rude jerk when I met you."

"And you were incredibly annoying. Still are, actually," he muttered.

"Excuse me?"

He sighed. "Nothing dear."

"Yeah, that's what I thought."

I grinned at them. "Are you always like this?"

"Yes," they replied in unison.

"It's why we get along so well," Hailey explained. "I don't let him get away with crap."

"And I keep her level when she has to be in a wheelchair," Blake added.

"Sounds like it works out well for you two. How did you meet?" I asked.

"At school. After my accident I went to live with my uncle and ended up going to the same school as Blake. I sat beside him in my first class and after a rough start, we became friends, and then eventually more." Hailey looked at him fondly. "He may be an ass, but he's my ass now."

Blake raised her left hand to his lips and kissed her knuckles. "And I always will be. Even though you're driving me nuts with these wedding details right now."

"I just want everything to be perfect."

"Hales, as long as you say 'I do' on that day then it'll be perfect. You don't need to worry about anything else."

"Easy for you to say, since you don't care if people have a good time. I'm only planning on getting married once, so I want to do it right." She leaned up to kiss his cheek. "It'll all be over in a few months, and then you never have to worry about it again."

I felt a hand cover mine, and I looked over to see Chase smiling at me. "I want to be them when we grow up," he murmured in my ear.

I chuckled. "Me too."

Hailey and Blake stayed with us for the next hour. Blake and Chase surprisingly seemed to get along fairly well. At one point, they went down to the cafeteria together, leaving me and Hailey alone. She smiled at me. "So how are you really doing?"

I shrugged. "I'm pissed off," I admitted. "Everything was going pretty well, and then this happened. I just started jumping with my horse again, and now this will set me back at least a month."

She lifted a brow. "You ride horses?"

"Yeah, I have since before I could walk." I hesitated for a moment. "Luke and I were on our way home from a horse show when we were in the accident. The horse I'm riding now used to be his, and I want to enter him in the first show of the season in memory of my brother."

"That's a really sweet thing for you to do. Do you think you'll be able to still do it?"

"I don't know. Jared hasn't been here yet, so I haven't talked to him about it."

"When you do talk to him, remember what I told you. Do everything he tells you to do. Do it twice if you can. It'll pay off in the end, even if it hurts like crazy at the time."

"I will. If it works out that I can go, will you come and watch me? I'd like for you to be there."

"Definitely. And I'd like to come meet your horse before, if you don't mind. I don't think I've ever really gotten close to one before, but it's something I've always wanted to do."

"Of course. As soon as they let me out of here, we'll arrange something." The boys came back into the room then. Blake had his hand on Chase's shoulder, and they moved over to us easily. Chase bent down to give me a kiss once Blake was safely beside Hailey again, and I smiled up at him. "Think you can ask the nurses if I can go for another walk? I'm not going to build up my strength again by just lying here."

"Sure, I'll be right back."

Hailey smiled at me and I settled back into my pillows with a new determination. I was going to compete in that show, no matter what.

# Chapter 18

My nightmares returned when I was released from the hospital. I never remembered what they were about, but after waking up screaming three nights in a row, I reluctantly started taking my sleeping pills again. I stopped having the nightmares, but the pills always left me feeling groggy for most of the morning, which I hated.

When school started up again, I was back on crutches. I wasn't happy about it, but I knew that I'd be back to my cane in another week or so, so I didn't let it bother me too much. The semester was starting to wind down, so final projects and exams became a bit of a worry. And it wasn't only my own projects that I had to worry about; Chase was going to be starting his project with Vicky Morgan tonight, and I knew I had to be there for him, no matter what my feelings were about her.

Chase took me straight to his place after school. Bev and Carson were still at work, so we had the house to ourselves until Vicky got there. Chase decided that spending that time in his bedroom was an acceptable pastime, and I couldn't say that I didn't agreed. We spent a pleasurable hour together, then got dressed again and grabbed a snack from the kitchen.

We moved into the living room and I stretched out on the couch with my notes so I could do some studying. Starlight settled himself contentedly on my stomach, and Chase sat with my feet in his lap.

When the doorbell rang, Chase groaned and reluctantly got to his feet. I heard him go to the front door and open it, and then a moment later, he came back in. He resumed his position with my feet in his lap while a girl with light brown hair and blue eyes came into the room. She was looking around curiously at everything, but her eyes narrowed when she saw me on the couch. "What are you doing here?" she asked snidely.

"Nice to see you to, Vicky," I replied drolly. "I'm here because I'm spending time with my boyfriend and our child."

Her brows winged up. "Child?"

I nodded solemnly and stroked the kitten that was still purring on my stomach. "This is Starlight. We adopted him a few weeks ago. I know it may seem a little soon, but we couldn't say no to his little face."

Chase snorted, but didn't say anything. Vicky just looked at me like I was on crack. "You are so weird," she muttered, before turning to Chase. "Should we get started on the project?"

He shrugged and glanced over at me. I smirked at him and then looked back at my book. "Just pretend I'm not here. It'd probably be easiest if you just gave Chase something to do, since it doesn't seem like he's going to talk to you."

Vicky sighed loudly before looking over the project outline. "Fine, you can just look up foods from the country we're researching."

Chase grabbed his laptop from the table beside the couch and placed it on my legs. He opened it and started typing into a search engine. I concentrated fully on my own book once more, and that's how we spent the next hour. My leg started to get stiff, so I shifted a little, trying to get into a more comfortable position without disturbing Starlight. When Chase looked over at me questioningly, I smiled apologetically. "My leg is cramping up," I explained.

Understanding lit his face, and he shut his laptop and put it beside the couch. Then he put both hands on my left leg and started to massage it gently. Slowly, the muscles loosened up, and I sighed and closed my eyes in appreciation. It had been weird the first couple of times that he had massaged my leg for me, but I was used to it by now.

He slid his hands under the leg of my jeans and pushed it up slightly so he could rub my skin. He was careful of the spot where I'd had surgery just under a week ago, but other than that he applied equal pressure everywhere.

I became so relaxed that I was nearly falling asleep when Vicky suddenly spoke up. I'd almost forgotten that she was there, since it had been so quiet in the room. "God, how can you touch that horrible thing?" she asked in disgust. "It's so gross!"

I automatically tried to pull my leg out of Chase's grip, but he refused to let go. I looked at his face, and the expression in his eyes had me swallowing back the words I'd been about to say. I'd only seen that look once or twice, but I knew him well enough to know by now that nothing good was going to happen now. I waited in tense silence for him to speak. When he did, he said only two words. "Get out."

Vicky's eyes widened and her jaw dropped. "What?"

Chase gently moved my feet off his lap and stood up, his whole body rigid with anger. "I said get out." His voice was low, but the anger in it was enough to send shivers down my spine. When Vicky just remained sitting with her mouth open, Chase's control snapped. "Get the hell out of my house!" he shouted.

That caused Vicky to jerk out of her stupor, and she scrambled to gather her things. A moment later, she scurried out of the room. The sound of the front door slamming reverberated through the house as Chase turned back to me. He knelt by my head and ran a finger down my cheek. "You okay?"

I nodded speechlessly and he went back to the end of the couch and resumed his previous position, minus the laptop. He stared off into space as he absently stroked my legs lightly. When I finally got over the shock of hearing him yell like that, I nudged him lightly with one foot. "Told you she didn't like me."

Chase turned his head to look at me with one brow raised. "You failed to mention that she's an evil bitch."

"Sorry, I thought that was implied," I said dryly. "What are you going to do now?"

He shrugged. "I'll just tell my teacher that I can't work with her. Either I'll get a different partner or I'll fail. I don't really care; there is no way in hell I am working with that girl again."

"I don't want you to fail," I murmured.

"Don't worry, I'll figure something out. Want to go get something to eat?"

I agreed and we spent the rest of the evening just relaxing and not doing anything related to school. I was a little worried about what would happen in Chase's class, but he seemed to be pretty laidback about it, so I decided to just wait and see what happened.

The next day, Chase was waiting for me outside the cafeteria and he was once again scowling. I brought him to the same stairwell as I had last time so I could talk to him. "How did it go?"

"I hate that teacher," he grumbled.

"Did he fail you?" He shook his head. "Are you stuck with Vicky?" Another head shake. "Then what happened?"

He crossed his arms over his chest. "I got paired with Adam."

I blinked a few times as I processed his words. "As in, my ex-boyfriend Adam?"

"Yes, that one," he snapped.

I stared at him for a minute before groaning and rubbing my hands over my face. "Now what do we do?"

He settled his hands on my hips and pulled me a little closer to him. "I don't know. It's going to be a little awkward."

I let out a humorless laugh. "That's putting it mildly." I peered up at his face. "Do you still want me to be there when you have to work on the project?"

Chase hesitated for a second before nodding. "Yeah, I don't want to do it without you." He sighed and dipped his head to give me a light kiss. "We'll figure it out tonight I guess. He's supposed to come over so we can work on it."

"Look on the bright side. At least we know he won't be an ass to me."

He snorted. "Oh yeah, I'll just have to worry about him having inappropriate thoughts about you. No big deal."

"Well, I'll only be having inappropriate thoughts about you. Doesn't that count for something?"

His lips tugged up into a reluctant smile and he kissed me again. "It counts for a lot," he murmured against my lips. His arms tightened around me, shuffling me closer until I was pressed against his body. He deepened the kiss and I wrapped my arms around him snugly.

A throat clearing had us springing apart, and I looked over my shoulder to see a teacher standing there with a disapproving frown. "None of that on school property," she scolded us.

Chase and I looked at each other and barely managed to keep straight faces as I hastily apologized. We moved past her, out of the stairwell, and went to the cafeteria to eat. My lips were still tingling from that kiss, and I saw Chase shoot me a few glances throughout the rest of the lunch period. I'm pretty sure Cindy noticed the looks as well, but she didn't say anything.

When the school day ended, Chase brought me to his house once again. We wasted no time going to his bedroom, just like yesterday. Only this time, the doorbell rang before we even had a chance to get all our clothes off. Chase looked at his watch and frowned. "Damn it, he's early."

"I'll get the door. You take a minute to… calm yourself down." I put my shirt back on hurriedly and grabbed my crutches. I made my way out of his room and to the front door. I opened it and gave Adam a small smile. "Hey."

"Hey," he responded. He looked me up and down, and then raised an eyebrow. "Did I interrupt something?"

I glanced down at myself and cursed when I realized my shirt was on inside out. "Um, maybe?" I said with a blush.

He rolled his eyes. "No need to be embarrassed. I remember what it's like."

I winced. "Uh, maybe don't say anything like that around Chase, okay? He's already not happy about having to work on this project with you."

"Don't worry; I have no desire to get into a fight with him. I have a feeling he'd win. Are you going to let me in?"

I stepped back to let him in and then closed the door behind him. I led him into the living room and a moment later, Chase came in while pulling his shirt back on. I saw Adam's expression waver slightly when he caught a glimpse of the scars on Chase's body, but luckily he didn't say anything. Chase came to my side and kissed the top of my head before leading me to the couch. I didn't have my history book this time, so I curled up beside him with the TV remote.

Adam sat in a chair to my right and pulled out his books. "So, I did some research with my other partner before we got switched around." He paused for a moment. "Why did we get switched, anyways? I don't even know who you were working with."

"Vicky Morgan," I replied. "She said something unpleasant to me yesterday and Chase kind of snapped."

Adam's expression turned icy. "What did she say?"

I shrugged. "It doesn't matter." Her comments had bothered me more than I'd let on, and I didn't want to talk about it.

Chase put a hand on my thigh and rubbed it gently. He brought his lips down to my ear. "I told you not to worry about what she said," he murmured.

I shivered as his warm breath blew against my ear. "It doesn't bother me," I lied. "I don't listen to anything she says anyways."

Adam regarded us curiously before turning his attention to Chase. "What did she say?"

Chase hesitated a moment. "She saw Dana's leg," he finally said.

Surprise and then understanding dawned on Adam's face. "I've never understood why she hates you so much, Dana."

"She had a crush on Luke, but he wouldn't give her the time of day. She decided to blame me for that, even though I had nothing to do with it." Starlight chose that moment to leap up onto my lap, so I concentrated on stroking him. "Look, can we just forget it? It's over and done with. You should work on your project."

I think Adam wanted to argue, but something in my expression must have deterred him, because he agreed and gave some papers to Chase for him to read. Much like yesterday, the time went by quietly, though I had the TV on this time. Chase kept touching me in small ways, and I think part of the reason he did it was because Adam was there. I was tempted to be a little annoyed about it, but I knew he was still a bit insecure about anything good in his life so I let it go.

After an hour of them working on their project, Adam said he had to get going. But before he left the room, he hesitated for a moment. "Dana, do you think I could talk to Chase alone for a minute?"

I raised my brows and opened my mouth to protest, but Chase cut me off. "It's okay. Why don't you go hang out in my room for a few minutes?"

I searched his face closely, but didn't detect any anger in him, so I agreed. I went to his room and five minutes later he came in as well. "What was that about?"

He sat beside me on his bed. "Maybe he's not as much of an ass as I originally thought," he mumbled grudgingly.

"What did he say to you?"

He lifted his head to look at me. "Basically he threatened to kill me if I hurt you."

"And that makes him less of an ass?" I asked incredulously.

He grinned. "Yeah."

"I will never understand guys," I muttered.

"You don't have to understand us," he replied. "Although there is one aspect of me that you should always know."

"Oh really? And what's that?"

Before I had a chance to react, he had me pinned to the bed. "I always finish what I start." He sealed his mouth over mine, effectively distracting me from my thoughts about how confusing men really are.

# Chapter 19

Three weeks after I was released from the hospital, I was ready to try riding Justice again. Chase came down to the stables with me and helped me get him ready. Once we were in the arena, I brought Justice over to the mounting block and got onto him. My left leg felt a little weaker than it had last time I'd rode him, but it wasn't too bad.

I didn't do a lot with him for that first ride. I mainly just walked him and did a little bit of trotting. I was pleased with how well my leg held up while riding him, and I was smiling when I slid off of him. "Your turn," I told Chase, holding out the helmet. "But you have to ride him around by yourself, since I can't walk all that well yet."

Chase let out a long suffering sigh, but I knew he was actually starting to like riding. He put the helmet on and I held Justice while he climbed on. Then I sat on the mounting block and gave him instructions while he rode him around the arena. I was pleasantly surprised at how well Justice did for Chase; before Luke had passed away, there was no was Justice would have been calm enough for this. But now he was laidback and listened to Chase really well.

When Chase was done riding him, we untacked him together and gave him some treats before going up to the house. My parents had gone out to dinner and a movie, so we had the house to ourselves. We decided to play a board game, so we set it up on the kitchen table. "I was thinking of inviting Blake and Hailey over here this weekend," I told him. "Hailey said she's always wanted to see horses up close. Does that sound like a good idea to you?"

He nodded. "They seemed like nice people. I wouldn't mind getting together with them."

"Good, then I'll call her tomorrow and set it up."

I did just that the next day, and Hailey was enthusiastic about coming over on Saturday. I said that they were also more than welcome to stay for dinner, and she was happy to agree to that.

Saturday dawned sunny but cold. Chase showed up first, and Blake and Hailey arrived shortly after. The four of us went down to the stables together. I was a little nervous, because this would be the first time I'd been to the stables during the daylight since the accident, and since it was Saturday, I knew it would be busy. I'd let my parents know what my plan was though, so they had everything set up for me in a slightly more private area of the barn.

I still had to go through the main part to get to it, though. I got quite a few surprised looks from everyone who saw me, but I didn't stop to talk to anyone. I led my little group past everyone to a stall that was usually empty, but had a horse in it today. A large black head appeared over the stall door, and I patted the horse lightly. "This is Autumn. He's a horse that's usually used for lessons, but my parents took him out of the rotation for us today. He's broke to drive, which means he pulls carts and sleighs. Since there's still a fair amount of snow on the ground, I thought you guys might like to go for a sleigh ride."

Hailey's eyes lit up. "That sounds like fun!"

"Good, I'll get him harnessed up then." My parents had left his harness by the stall, so I brushed him quickly and then got him ready to go. Once the harness was on, I led him out of the stall and down the aisle. Chase walked beside me while Hailey and Blake followed along behind. When we were outside again, I hooked Autumn up to the sleigh, then helped Hailey and Blake get settled in. Chase sat beside me and I gathered up the reins and clucked, causing Autumn to set off at a walk.

I guided him down a nicely groomed trail, and the four of us chatted as we went along. "So Autumn is a lesson horse?" Hailey asked.

"Yeah, he's used for a lot of beginners. He's big, but he's also very gentle and listens really well. We got him about five years ago and everyone loves him. He's a favorite at the barn."

"How many students are there here?"

"I think around sixty or seventy, but that doesn't include boarders. Most of them take lessons on their own horses."

"You grew up here?" she wanted to know.

"Born and raised," I replied. "I can't imagine living anywhere else."

"You're so lucky. I grew up in town, but I always loved visiting friends who lived in the country. There's just so much… space out here."

I smiled. "Yeah, there definitely is. I don't think I'd ever be able to live in a town." I clucked and tapped the reins on Autumn's rump to get him into a trot. "So when are you two getting married?"

"In August," she responded. "Blake wanted to get married earlier, but I told him planning a wedding takes time."

"If we'd just eloped like I suggested, we wouldn't have had to worry about all this crap," Blake grumbled. "Who really cares what kind of flowers we're having? Or if the invitations look to plain? We're the ones getting married, not everyone else."

"Oh stop being such a grump," Hailey chided. "This means a lot to me."

Blake sighed. "I know, which is why I agreed to wait until you could plan this whole thing. I'm just impatient to be married to you."

"How long have you two been together?" I asked.

"Four years. We met in our final year of high school. We actually went to the same school that you go to now," Hailey said.

"Really? That's kind of cool. It's a nice school."

"Is Mr. Avery still the principal there?"

"Yeah. He's a nice guy."

"He is," Hailey agreed. "Blake and I had trouble with a substitute teacher there one day, and Mr. Avery made sure that he was forced to retire after that."

This intrigued me. "What happened?"

She went on to explain how the teacher had been incredibly rude to them and wouldn't let them explain that Blake was blind, which was why they'd been working together. "Mr. Avery said it was obvious that the teacher was in the wrong, which surprised me at first. But the more I got to know him, the more I realized that he's really an awesome principal. He helped us plan a surprise for a talent show at the school. Blake and I performed and caught everyone completely by surprise. It was pretty cool."

"What did you perform?"

"I played the piano and sang, and Blake played the guitar and sang."

"That's great! Do you guys still play?"

"Blake teaches guitar now, so he plays all the time. We do perform occasionally still, but usually only for a good cause. We were on the Eve McGill show once. There's also a video of us on YouTube."

"I am definitely going to check it out when I get home," I told them.

We spent the next hour going along a bunch of the trails that twined through the forest. I had a lot of fun with them, and Chase even joined in on the conversation a little bit. They stayed for dinner and my parents seemed to like both of them and invited them to come back anytime they wanted.

Once they had left for the evening, Chase and I went onto the computer and searched YouTube for the video of them. We found it and sat in silence as we watched it. "Wow, they're really good," I said after the video ended.

"They are," Chase agreed. "It's weird seeing Hailey in a wheelchair."

"It is. But she did say that this was taken shortly after she slipped and fell on the ice. You wouldn't know anything was wrong with her today if you didn't know her situation." I glanced down at my leg. "Makes me hope that maybe one day I'll be able to walk without a cane again."

Chase leaned in and kissed my cheek. "Jared said that might happen, right?"

"Yeah, but I didn't really believe him before. Now maybe I do."

"If you set your mind to it, anything is possible."

I raised an eyebrow. "Since when are you so philosophical?"

"Since I realized that it doesn't matter how hard your life has been in the past. You can still shape how it turns out in the future. Just look at Blake and Hailey. Both of them had huge obstacles to overcome, but they managed to do it and they're obviously very much in love. It kind of makes me think that maybe we'll be like them when we're older."

"So you think I'll keep you around that long?" I asked teasingly.

"Of course. I'm too cute for you to ditch me."

I laughed and leaned my head on his shoulder. "You're probably right."

He left about half an hour later, and I got ready for bed. Once I was curled up under the covers, I realized I'd forgotten to take my sleeping pill, but I was too comfortable to bother getting up and taking it. With the great day I'd had, I figured I'd be able to sleep without any nightmares.

I was wrong. I dreamt about the accident like I always did, but there was something different about the ending that I never remembered when I woke up. Only this time, I did remember. I remembered something that my brain had obviously repressed after the accident. And when I woke up with my heart pounding and a scream caught in my throat, I wished with all my heart that it had stayed like that.

# Chapter 20

I retreated into myself over the next couple of days. I refused to go to school and I stopped talking once again. I remained in my room, not even leaving to get something to eat. My parents became frantic with worry, and Chase was completely bewildered by the change in my attitude. I would curl up against him when he came to see me, but I wouldn't even talk to him.

After three days of this, he'd finally had enough. "Damn it Dana, tell me what the hell happened!"

My eyes snapped open in shock at the tone of his voice. So far he'd been quiet and understanding, not pushing me into anything. But now he'd obviously lost his patience. "There's nothing to tell," I said, my voice raspy from lack of use.

"Bullshit. Three days ago you were perfectly fine. We had a great time with Blake and Hailey and you were happy when I left you. The next morning, you turned into a shell of a person. What happened?"

"I had a nightmare," I whispered.

He rubbed my back gently. "Okay, what was it about?"

"The crash."

He frowned. "I thought that's what they were always about." When I nodded, he laid his hand on my cheek. "What was different about it?"

My breath hitched as I turned away from him. "I remembered something."

He sighed and forced me to look at him again. "What did you remember?" When I didn't answer, he framed my face with both hands. "Dana, please tell me. This is killing me."

It was only then that I realized how pale he looked, and he had circles under his eyes. "The accident happened so quickly," I said. "One minute we were driving along, and the next we had a car slamming into us. I remember Luke looking over at me just before we were hit. The look in his eyes is one I'll always remember from now on. There was a lot of fear in them, but there was also a brief flash of determination. A moment before the car crashed into us, Luke jerked the steering wheel to the right, causing his car to veer to the side a little." I paused and placed a hand on my leg. "If he hadn't done that, I would've been killed." I don't know how I knew that, but I did.

"He saved your life," Chase said quietly.

I was jerked back to the present by his words. "And in exchange, he lost his," I said bitterly. "He should've just let the car hit us like it was supposed to. Then he'd still be alive, and I wouldn't."

"You don't mean that," Chase said warily.

"Yes I do. Luke was a much better person than I was. It should've been him that survived, not me."

Chase suddenly got to his feet. "I'm not going to listen to this." He turned and left the room without another word.

I watched him go, mildly shocked but not really able to make myself care. I curled back up on my bed and waited for sleep to take over once again.

I didn't see Chase again for two days. My parents had finally cajoled me into eating, but I only picked at my food. I still remained in my room for most of the time and I refused to go down to the barn. It felt like everything I'd been trying to live for no longer mattered.

I was lying on my bed in the evening when I heard my door open and someone came in. I didn't think anything of it until a folder was suddenly dropped in front of my face. I raised my eyes and saw Chase standing there with his arms crossed over his chest. "What's this?" I asked.

"Open it," he replied.

I sat up and pulled the folder into my lap. I opened it and my brows winged up. "A police report?"

"Yeah, the one that was written about your accident."

I lifted my eyes to his again. "How did you get this?"

"Remember the cop I told you about that found me when I was younger? Well, he pulled some strings and got this for me. Read it."

I set the folder down. "I don't want to."

"Fine, then I'll tell you what it says." He sat down beside me and picked up the folder, but he didn't open it. "It says if the car you were in had been hit completely head on, you would have been killed instantly. Since it hit at an angle, your leg was crushed, but you somehow survived."

"I already know that," I said.

He narrowed his eyes at me. "I'm not done," he said coolly. "I talked to the officers who responded to the scene. I asked them if Luke would have survived if the car had been hit head on. You know what they said?" When I didn't answer, he continued. "They said that there was no way he could've survived. The airbag on his side of the vehicle was defective and didn't go off. The steering wheel crushed his chest, which is what killed him. If he hadn't jerked the steering wheel at the last minute, it wouldn't have mattered. Even if the airbag had worked, there was a ninety percent chance that he would've been killed because of how the car was built. The fact that you survived is a miracle, because both the officers said that you should've been killed as well."

I was quiet for a moment as I absorbed all of this. "So we would've both died if he hadn't done that," I said quietly. "I wished for that so often right after I woke up. At least then I'd be with him."

"So this is how you repay him? He saved your life, Dana. He somehow knew in that split second that he needed to save you. You've told me about the bond that the two of you always had. Do you really think he'd want you to be with him right now?"

Tears pooled in my eyes and slowly trickled down my cheeks. "No," I whispered. "He would want me to live."

Chase wrapped his arms around me and pulled me onto his lap. "Then do what he wanted you to do. Live."

I buried my face in his chest and sobbed quietly. It was a relief to let the emotions out that I'd kept penned up for the last five days. When I had quieted down, I raised my tearstained face up so I could look at the young man I loved. "Thank you."

"I love you, Dana. I'll do anything for you."

"But you left me."

"No I didn't. I was here for the past two days; you were always just sleeping. And it wasn't easy getting this report for you."

I laid my head on his should and let out a shuddering breath. "I thought I was finally getting better when it came to thinking of Luke. Now I don't know what to feel."

"You can feel however you want. But keep in mind what you think he'd want you to do with your life. I didn't know him, but from what you've told me I don't think he'd want you to mourn him forever. He'd want you to move on."

"How did you get so smart?" I asked him.

He smiled and brushed my hair off my cheek. "I started hanging out with you," he said. "You've made me look at life in a different way; now I'm just trying to repay the favor."

"Will you come down to see Justice with me?"

"Of course. Let's go grab our coats."

It was silent in the barn when we entered it, but as soon as Justice heard my cane tapping on the concrete of the aisle, he whinnied and stuck his head over the door. My heart contracted a little and I picked up the pace until I was outside at his door. "Hey boy. Did you miss me?" He snorted and pushed his head into my chest. I smiled a little and ran my fingers through his forelock. "I missed you too," I murmured. "Sorry I kind of disappeared for a few days."

Chase came up behind me and slid his arms around my waist. "Are you going to take him for a ride?"

I shook my head. "Not tonight. I'm a little weaker than usual since I haven't been eating or doing a lot for the past little while. I'll get my strength back up and then I'll start riding him again."

"Well, do you want to give me a riding lesson then?"

I turned to face him and looked up at his face. "Are you trying to distract me?"

"That depends. Is it working?"

"Yeah, it is. Let's get Autumn tacked up for you. I want to get you to do more tonight, but I don't think you're ready to do it with Justice."

He groaned. "What am I getting myself into?"

I ignored his grumbling and we went over to Autumn's stall. I helped Chase get the horse ready and then we went into the arena. "Okay, I'm going to sit on the mounting block while you ride. All this walking has tired me out."

He stopped and turned to look at me in concern. "Are you okay?"

"Yeah, just a little weak. I'll be okay." There was more meaning in those last three words than anything else I'd said that night.

Chase sighed and stroked my cheek once before grudgingly going to the mounting block and climbing onto Autumn. "Ugh, this guy is a lot wider than Justice."

I grinned. "That's because he's part Percheron, while Justice is a Danish Warmblood. There's a bit of a difference."

He gave me a dry look. "You do know that what you just said is practically gibberish to me, right?"

I chuckled a little. "I know. Autumn and Justice are different breeds of horses. Understand?"

"Ah, okay. So, what do I do?"

I settled into instructor mode as Chase rode the horse around the arena. By the end, I had him trotting around a little, which I thought was a pretty big accomplishment, considering Chase had been reluctant to start riding in the first place. Once we were done with the lesson, Chase went to untack Autumn while I went back to Justice's stall. I let myself in and put my arms around his neck.

"Well boy, looks like we're going to have to start training harder. I want to do well in that show so that when Luke looks down at us from heaven, he'll be proud. That okay with you?" He sighed heavily and I smiled. "Don't worry; I think I'll be working harder than you. At least you have four good legs, whereas I only have one."

I heard Chase coming down the aisle, so I released Justice and stepped out of the stall. Chase put his arm around my waist as we started back up to the house. "You ready to start living again?" he asked.

I looked up at the clear night sky and felt a sense of peace settle over me. "Oh yeah, I'm ready."

# Chapter 21

I threw myself into training. Now that I had remembered that Luke had saved my life, I had even more reason to want to be ready for this show. I rode Justice almost every night, only giving us one night off a week. My leg became a lot stronger, but I still needed my cane. I didn't let that bother me though; I was just happy that I was improving.

Chase came with me to the barn whenever he could. I gave him lessons at least three nights a week, and he started getting pretty good. He became more comfortable on horses and he really seemed to like riding Autumn.

The weather improved over the next three months, and I finally started riding during the day again, so that I could work with Justice outside. I usually only rode when no one else was around still, but sometimes people would see me and stop to watch. I knew my parents must have talked to everyone though, because no one ever questioned me.

On a beautiful day in early May, I met Chase down at the barn. We were going to go on our first trail ride today, and I had packed a picnic lunch for us, which was currently in the backpack I had on. We got Justice and Autumn ready to go, and then mounted up and headed out.

"So the show's next weekend. How are you feeling?" Chase asked me.

"Nervous," I admitted. "But I think we're ready."

He glanced over at me. "Well, I'm not an expert, but the two of you look more than ready to me."

I smiled. "We do seem to work well together. I'm more worried about seeing all the people at the show than actually riding in it."

"Do you think any of them will bug you?"

I shook my head. "No; it'll just be strange, that's all. I haven't seen any of them in a year and it's a pretty close knit group of people for the most part. I don't really know what to expect."

"I'll be with you the whole time," he promised.

"I know, and that makes it all a little less nerve-wracking," I told him. "Come on, let's trot a little bit."

We followed one of my favorite trails and eventually ended up in a clearing that was filled with wildflowers. We got off the horses and tied them up before settling on the ground. I opened my backpack and started pulling food out. Chase's eyebrows rose when he saw how much I had packed. "Are we expecting company out here or something?"

I gave him a sheepish look. "No, I just kind of went a little crazy when I was making food. I was excited about coming out here today."

He laughed and helped me unpack the rest. "Well we won't starve, that's for sure," he teased me.

I stuck my tongue out at him. "Just shut up and eat," I said.

We dug into the food, eating as much of it as we could. When we were done, we packed it back up and then stretched out on the ground. I laid my head on Chase's chest and gazed out over the field. "Luke and I used to come here every year the weekend before this show. It helped remind us that showing and winning isn't everything. The moments spent out here with our horses are more important than any ribbons we may win."

"You used to trail ride with him a lot?"

"Yeah, every other weekend when the weather was nice if we could. We'd usually bring a lunch like we did today, and we'd sit out here and tell each other anything that was going on in our lives. It was on a day like this that I first told him that Adam asked me out."

"What did he say?"

I chuckled a little. "He wasn't entirely impressed by the idea. The three of us had kind of been friends for a few years, and Luke was a little pissed that Adam would do that. He was relieved when I told him that I'd turned Adam down."

"And what was Luke's reaction when you finally said yes?"

"He was actually okay with it. I guess he had talked to Adam about it, and after some crazy threats on my brother's part, they came to an understanding. I don't know if Luke was ever entirely comfortable with it, but he never bugged me about it." I paused. "Well, not too much anyways."

Chase ran his fingers through my hair. "Do you think he would have liked me?"

I thought about it for a few minutes. "I don't know," I said slowly. "He would've liked you as a person, I think. But if he saw how close you and I were, he might have had a problem with it. He once told me that part of the reason he didn't mind me being with Adam was because he knew it would likely only be a teenager thing." I smiled a little. "I got really mad at him for saying that. At that time, I believed that I would be with Adam forever. Now I know that it wouldn't have lasted, but that's not the point. The point is, I think Luke would know that this is a lot different. He'd probably have more of a problem with it, because he'd be afraid of losing me."

"I never would have taken you away from him," Chase protested.

I shifted so I could look at his face. "Not intentionally, you wouldn't have. But Luke was always a little jealous when I spent time with someone away from him. I was the same way. I hated it when he would go out with friends without me."

"Really? Why?"

I sighed. "It's hard to explain. Luke and I always had to be near each other. We couldn't spend more than a couple of days apart without feeling sick. I think it was an ingrained fear that every time one of us went out with someone, it would take us away from each other. Does that make sense?"

"I think so," Chase replied. "Maybe that's another reason Luke didn't mind you being with Adam. If you were all friends, he knew you'd be able to hang out together."

I considered it. "I never thought about it like that, but you might be right."

"Did he ever have any girlfriends?"

I snorted and rolled my eyes. "Luke didn't do 'girlfriends'. He always said that he had too much love to give out to settle on just one girl. He always had girls flocking around him, so he could have had his pick. But he preferred to just have casual flings and nothing else."

"Sounds like every teenage boy's hero," Chase said. When I raised an eyebrow, he smiled charmingly. "Aside from myself, of course."

"Oh yeah, of course," I replied dryly. I glanced at my watch. "Let's head back. It's getting late and we promised Hailey and Blake that we would have dinner with them, remember?"

"I remember. They're still planning on coming to the show, right?"

"Yeah, Hailey seems really excited about it. I don't know if Blake is looking forward to it or not, though. He's kind of hard to read sometimes."

"He is," Chase agreed. "But I like him."

"So do I." I got to my feet. "Let's get going."

The night before we would be leaving for the show, I was watching a movie with Chase. He was staying the night tonight, since we were planning on leaving early in the morning. Normally we would be leaving in the evening, but my parents wanted to get there before the rush, so we were taking the day off of school tomorrow.

While we were curled up on the couch, I suddenly got the feeling someone else was in the room, but when I looked around, no one was there. I sat up straight when I realized that this was exactly like how I'd felt the first time I went down to see Justice after the accident. As soon as I was sitting up straight, I felt that tugging at my soul again and I got to my feet.

"Dana? What are you doing?" Chase asked me.

"Luke wants me to do something."

Most people would have looked at me like I was nuts, but Chase just got to his feet as well. "Okay, what is it?"

I started moving forward until I got to the bottom of the stairs in the hallway. I looked over at Chase. "Give me a ride up?"

Instead of giving me a piggy back ride like he usually did, he scooped me up into his arms and carried me to the top. "Now where?" he wanted to know, keeping me in his arms.

I looked down at the end of the hallway, and a slight feeling of dread settled in the pit of my stomach. "I think I'm supposed to go in his room."

Chase hesitated only briefly before carrying me to the room I'd indicated and setting me down in front of it. "Do you want me to stay out here?"

I shook my head. "No, I want you to come in with me." I reached forward and grasped the doorknob. I let out a long breath and then slowly opened the door.

Everything looked the same as it had a year ago when I'd been in here. The bed was unmade, with one of the pillows thrown on the floor. His bedside table was cluttered with random things, but the picture of me and him was still there. There were a few articles of clothing scattered around on the floor, but I ignored all of that as I cautiously went inside. The tugging urged me over to his dresser, and there sitting on top of it was his lucky stock pin.

I gazed down at the horse-shaped piece of gold, and re-membered when I had given it to him when we were ten. I had saved up my allowance for months so I could buy it for him for our birthday. He'd been so happy when he opened it that I'd decided it was worth all the ice cream I'd missed being able to buy.

A tear tracked down my cheek as I reached down and picked up the pin. "This was his lucky stock pin," I told Chase in a low voice. "I bought it for him when we were ten. He wore it to every single show and any time he won he said it was because of this pin. If he didn't win, he would say it was because he hadn't believed in the power of the pin." I smiled a little. "I always told him that he was nuts, but he refused to show if he didn't have this with him."

"What are you going to do with it?"

I turned around to face him, closing my fist around the pin. "I'm going to wear it this weekend."

"Did he have it with him at that last show?"

I nodded. "He did. I wonder how it ended up back on his dresser. My parents never told me that they still had it; I think they would've given it to me if they did."

Chase slid his arms around my waist and pulled me in for a hug. "Maybe Luke didn't want it to be found until now."

I rested my cheek against his heart. "Maybe you're right." The pin was warm in my hand, and I smiled a little. I knew that my brother was wishing me luck at the show, and I was determined to believe in the power of the pin, just like he always did.

# Chapter 22

It was barely starting to get light out when the alarm in the motel room went off. Chase grunted and blindly smacked out at the offending piece of technology, swearing quietly when he only managed to knock it to the ground without shutting it off. He untangled himself from me and clambered out of the bed so he could finally silence the annoying beeping.

I sat up and watched in amusement as he stumbled into the bathroom. The only other time we'd spent the night together, he hadn't been so uncoordinated in the morning. When I glanced at the clock, I realized that it might be because it was only five thirty in the morning. I was used to early mornings for horse shows, though it had been a year since I'd been up at this time.

When Chase came back out of the bathroom, he looked slightly more alert. He raised an eyebrow when he saw me sitting up. "You look more awake than should be possible at this time of the morning."

I smiled. "This is nothing. There are some shows that I had to get up at three in the morning for."

He shuddered. "That's still the middle of the night."

I laughed as I climbed out of the bed. "I'll make sure to leave you out of those shows then," I teased him.

Before I could walk by him to go to the bathroom, he wrapped his arms around me. "Not a chance. I'll be with you for every show that you go to."

I tilted my head and kissed the tip of his nose. "You might change your mind by the time the day is over."

He kissed me lightly and then released me. "We'll see."

That first day went by pretty quickly. I had only entered Justice in one division, which consisted of two classes today, and then the championship round tomorrow. Justice and I did pretty well, only taking down one rail in each class. That allowed us to move onto the next day. Since there were over a hundred people in my division the first day, no one really paid too much attention to us. The number had been diminished to twenty-five for tomorrow though, so I had a feeling it might be a little different.

When Chase and I got back to the motel room that night, I was more tired than I had been in a long time, and my leg was pretty sore. Chase ran a bath for me, and then massaged my leg before we went to bed.

The next morning we arrived at the show grounds and went immediately to where Justice was stabled. I touched up his braids, since he'd rubbed some of them out overnight. Chase helped me by handing me the yarn when I needed it, and keeping Justice entertained so he didn't move too much.

My class wasn't until the afternoon, so once Justice was braided perfectly again, Chase and I found some seats so we could watch the main event of the show, which was just below the grand prix level. I noticed that a girl sitting near us kept glancing over at me, and she looked vaguely familiar, but she didn't approach us. It was almost as if she was waiting for something, but nothing happened and eventually she frowned a little and walked away.

My stomach was in knots by the time my class was ready to start. Chase boosted me up onto Justice's back, then stepped back as I went to the warm-up ring. I put Justice through his paces and hopped him over a couple of practice jumps, before bringing him back over to Chase. We watched the first few competitors go through the course, and none of them went clear. I was ninth to go in, and when I was on deck, I took a deep breath and looked down at Chase. "This is it."

He squeezed my leg reassuringly. "You can do this."

"I hope so," I muttered.

"Hey, you know you can. Luke is watching you right now and telling you to believe in the power of the pin."

My lips tugged up into a reluctant smile. "You're probably right." I leaned down and kissed him gently. "See you in a few minutes."

My number was called, and I gathered my reins up and urged Justice into the ring. I rode him to the middle of the ring and halted him, causing a few people in the crowd to murmur questioningly. The PA system crackled once and then the announcer's voice flowed out of the speakers.

"This is number two forty-seven, Dana Webster riding Luke's Justice. Dana is dedicating this ride to her brother, Luke, who was killed in a car accident one year ago. Many people at this show will remember that both Luke and Dana rode in this show last year. On their way home, their car was struck by a drunk driver. Dana is now riding Luke's horse in his memory. Before she begins, she's asked that everyone take a moment of silence to remember Luke."

The crowd was completely silent, and I reached up to rub the pin that was attached to my collar. A feeling of peace rushed through me, and I suddenly knew with certainty that Luke really was watching over me. The speakers crackled once more, and then the song "I believe I can Fly" by R Kelly came on.

I inhaled deeply once more and then squeezed Justice into a canter. I looked for my first jump, and turned him towards it. The course consisted of fifteen obstacles, scattered over a complex pattern. We cantered up to the first one, a deceptively simple vertical, and hopped over it neatly. We turned left and headed for an oxer next, which he also cleared easily. The next jump was a liverpool, which meant there was a blue tarp underneath it to simulate water. Justice didn't even bat an eye as he leapt nimbly over it.

A wall, two oxers and three verticals followed the liverpool, and then we reached the triple combination. This was one of the biggest trouble spots on the course, because the three jumps were only separated by two strides each. You had to hit it perfectly to get the right striding, or else you would knock one of the jumps down.

We came into the first one and cleared it without a problem. We took two strides, and Justice gathered himself to leap. He took off and fumbled slightly when he realized the jump was an oxer instead of a vertical. He managed to clear it, but we landed further out than we should have. He took one stride and launched into the air half a stride away from the final jump of the combination.

I clutched his mane and held my breath as we hung in the air. The jump was an oxer, making it wide on its own. With the distance we had added with the takeoff, I was expecting to crash through the jump.

When we hit the ground, I looked back briefly in complete surprise. The back pole wobbled once, but then settled back into its cups. I turned my head back to face forward, not entirely sure how we had cleared that. I concentrated on the next four jumps, and we cleared all of them. We crossed the finish line, and I brought him to a halt, sitting in stunned silence as the crowd erupted into cheers.

We had gone clear. There were still sixteen more competitors to go, so there was a high chance someone else would do that as well, but we were the first ones to do so. A feeling of elation settled over me and I leaned down to hug Justice around the neck before sitting up again and leaving the ring.

I slid off of Justice and into Chase's arms. He lifted me up in a power hug and then kissed me enthusiastically. "You did it!"

I laughed as he set me back onto my feet. "I thought for sure that the final part of that combination was going to come down."

"It was close," Chase admitted. "But Justice came through. Now what happens?"

"I'll be in a jump-off with whoever else goes clear," I told him. "It'll be a shorter time limit and not as many jumps. We just have to wait and see who else is in it."

As it turned out, no one else went clear. The liverpool and triple combination claimed most of the horses, but one rider did manage to get through without hitting anything. Unfortunately for them, they were a little too slow and came in over the time allowed. Since I was the only one who went clear under the time allowed, I won the class.

Chase hugged me tightly again and boosted me back onto Justice so I could claim my ribbon. The crowd gave me a standing ovation and I felt tears fill my eyes, since I knew they were cheering for Luke as well as for me. I accepted my ribbon and allowed the photographer from the local paper to take a picture of us.

Once that was done, Chase and I brought Justice back to his stall. My parents and Cindy were there to congratulate me, along with Blake and Hailey. Blake shocked me by hugging me, and even Hailey seemed surprised by it. Blake must have felt us staring at him in surprise, because he shrugged as he stepped back. "What? She did really well."

Hailey shook her head. "Never thought I'd see the day where he wasn't an ass to someone besides me."

Blake grinned charmingly at her. "Just trying to keep you on your toes, dear."

I laughed and laced my fingers with Chase's. "You guys are meeting us for dinner after the show is over, right?" We were planning on staying one more night and then leaving in the morning.

"Yeah, we'll meet you at the restaurant around seven. We'll be leaving to go home after that," Hailey replied.

We all chatted for a few more minutes, and then everyone aside from Chase left and we worked together to unbraid and untack Justice. I made him a bran mash afterwards and made sure he was comfortable. Then I just leaned on the stall door and looked in at him. Chase joined me and put his arm around my shoulders. "How are you feeling?" he asked.

"Happy," I replied. "And lighter than I've felt in a long time."

He kissed my temple. "Good, I'm glad."

We watched Justice in silence for a few minutes before we were interrupted. "Dana?" a voice asked uncertainly.

I turned and saw the girl that had been looking at us earlier standing a few feet away. "Yes?" I noticed that she looked a little paler now than she had earlier, and I was a little concerned that she was going to pass out.

"My name is Cara. We met briefly last year at this show."

I frowned and thought back to that last show. It suddenly dawned on me where I'd seen her. "Oh! You were hanging out with Luke that weekend."

She blushed slightly. "Yeah. I was here to watch my cousin ride, even though I've never really had an interest in horses. Luke kept me company and made it more bearable."

I vaguely remembered Luke telling me about her. "That sounds like something he'd be good at."

"I- I didn't know anything had happened to him," she said quietly. "I came here this year to find him."

"Oh," I responded. I didn't know what else to say to her.

She hesitated for a minute. "When he never called me, I was so mad at him. I never imagined that he had been in an accident."

"He would've called you," I said awkwardly. "Luke was a good guy."

She blew out a breath. "This is a lot harder than I knew it was going to be," she muttered, almost to herself. Then she squared her shoulders. "You and him were twins, right? I remember him telling me how close the two of you were."

My heart clenched. "Yeah, we were twins. When he died, I lost part of myself."

She nodded. "Well, the reason I wanted to find Luke was to tell him that I became pregnant that weekend last year."

My jaw dropped and I stared at her for a full minute before I was able to say anything. "What?"

She blushed again. "I'm not normally the kind of girl that will sleep with a guy she just met, but there was something different about Luke. I went to his motel room with him and well... I ended up getting pregnant."

My mind was whirling as I processed this. "Luke... Luke has a kid?"

Cara took out her phone and fiddled with it for a few minutes before turning it to show me a picture. "His name is Matthew. He's three months old."

I stared at the picture of the smiling baby and it felt like I'd been kicked in the stomach. The baby looked like a miniature Luke. "Oh my God."

Chase stepped forward and wrapped his arm around my waist. "Breathe Dana," he murmured in my ear.

I inhaled shakily, only now realizing that I'd stopped breathing momentarily. "He looks just like him," I said, still staring at the photo.

Chase looked down at the picture. "He does," he agreed.

I tore my eyes away from the photo and looked back at Cara. "Where is he?"

"With my parents right now. I was planning on giving him up for adoption, but the further I got into the pregnancy the more I realized I couldn't do that. My mom helps me with him a lot. They weren't happy with me when they found out I was pregnant, but they supported everything I decided."

"Do they know who the father is?"

She shook her head. "I wanted to tell Luke first. When he didn't call, I finally decided to just call him. But his phone was disconnected, and I was so mad at him that I wouldn't tell anyone who he was. I did put his name on the birth certificate though. I was planning on confronting him today. When I saw you, I kept looking for him but never found him. It wasn't until I heard what the announcer said that I realized something had happened."

"He would've been there for you and Matthew," I told her with utmost sincerity. "He was the kind of guy who would've taken responsibility."

Cara sighed and put her phone away. "I got that feeling when I was with him, which is why I was so mad when I couldn't get in touch with him."

"I can't believe he has a kid," I said. "It's surreal."

Cara hesitated for a moment. "Would you like to meet him sometime?"

I hesitated for only a moment before nodding. "Yeah, I'd very much like that."

She gave me her number and we set up a time to meet next weekend. When she left, I sat down on a chair that was set up outside Justice's stall and put my head in my heads. "Wow."

Chase crouched in front of me and moved my hands. "That's one way to put it."

"I'm an auntie," I stated. "That is so weird."

"Look at it this way; now you'll always have a little piece of Luke."

"I didn't really think of it like that," I admitted. Then I grinned. "I always told him that this was going to happen one day." I shook my head. "I wonder what he's thinking up in heaven right now."

"He's probably panicking like any new dad would do," Chase replied dryly. "At least he doesn't have to worry about child support."

I snorted. "That's true. Fate works in mysterious ways, doesn't it?"

"It really does," he agreed. He kissed me lightly and then straightened up, pulling me to my feet. "What do you think your parents are going to say?"

I groaned. "Damn it, I have to be the one to tell them, don't I?"

He grinned. "Oh yeah."

I sighed and started to walk away from the stall. "Let's go tell them then. I'm glad I'm sharing a room at the motel with you; they are going to be pissed."

He chuckled and took my hand. "I love you," he stated.

I looked up at him as we walked. "I know. But if you get me pregnant, I'm going to have to kill you."

He laughed out loud at that and stopped so he could pick me up and spin me around. "I'll do my best not to do that then," he promised.

I grinned down at him. "Then I guess I love you too."

The sun shone down brightly on us as we headed over to his car, and a small breeze ruffled my hair. I smiled and looked up at the sky. "Don't worry little brother; I'll always love you as well and I'll watch over your little boy."

# Chapter 23

"Dana, are you ready to go?" Chase asked me as he came into our room.

I turned away from the mirror. "Just about. I can't get my locket on."

Chase came forward and took it from me, then turned me until my back was to him. He slipped the chain around my neck and did the clasp up. "There. Now are you ready?"

"Yeah, just need my shoes." I walked over to wear they were sitting on the bed, and I sat down to put them up. When they were on, I stood up once again. "Now I'm ready."

He swept an admiring gaze over me. "You look pretty hot," he stated.

"So do you," I replied. We were both all dressed up to go to Blake and Hailey's wedding.

"Now that we both know we look smoking, let's get out of here."

I laughed and looped my arm through his as we left the room. My parents were in the living room, and they made us stop so they could take pictures. Then we were allowed to leave, so Chase and I went out to his car. I didn't have my can anymore, and I was incredibly happy about that. I still walked with a limp, but it was getting harder and harder to notice as the days went by.

Chase held my door open for me and then shut it once I was sitting. He went around the car and climbed into the driver's seat. "We're still supposed to go spend the day with Cara and Matthew tomorrow, aren't we?" he asked as he started the car.

I smiled when I thought of my nephew. "Yeah; I can't wait to see him again. He looks more like Luke every day."

"He is a little cutie," he admitted, pulling onto the road.

"I'm glad Cara is letting us be in his life. She didn't have to tell me about him when she found out Luke had died, but she did. That says a lot about her."

"It does," Chase agreed. "I can't believe how much he has grown in the past three months."

"I know! Every time I see him it's like he's a different baby. And Cara said he's crawling now. I bet she has a hard time keeping up with him now that he's mobile."

"Are your parents coming with us tomorrow?"

"Not this time," I replied. "They'll come next weekend though." After their initial shock over being grandparents, my parents had quickly warmed to the idea and they now spoiled Matthew rotten. They were already planning on getting him his own pony when he was old enough.

We drove for a little while in silence. I looked out at the scenery, glad it was a nice day for the wedding since it was outdoors. I was looking forward to seeing Blake and Hailey again; they'd been pretty busy the last few weeks with last minute plans, so we hadn't gotten together as much as we usually did.

We arrived at the park where the wedding was taking place and found a parking spot pretty quickly. I clasped Chase's hand once we were both out of the car and we made our way to the seating area. The ceremony was due to start in half an hour, so we settled in to wait.

When the ceremony began, I couldn't help the few tears that escaped my eyes. I was so happy for the two of them and I knew that they were perfect for each other. Chase handed me a tissue without saying anything, and I discreetly wiped my eyes.

When the ceremony was over, we moved to the tent where the reception was being held. We'd only been sitting for five minutes when someone came up to us. "Are you Dana and Chase?" he asked, a harried look on his face. When we nodded, he looked relieved. "Good. I'm Liam, Hailey's uncle. She wants you to be in some pictures."

I looked at him in surprise. "But it's usually only the family and wedding party in pictures."

"She insisted that I find you guys and bring you over. There was no way I was going to try and tell her no."

We followed him back outside, and Hailey's face lit up when she saw us. "There you are! Come on, I want a picture of the four of us."

Chase and I posed for some pictures with them, and then waited until the photographer was done with everyone. Then we went back into the tent so Blake and Hailey could make their entrance. Once they had, the meal was served and everyone dug in.

After the traditional bouquet and garter toss, they had everyone clear the dance floor so that they could have their first dance. As the first bars of "I Run to You" by Lady Antebellum came on, I grinned. "Somehow I knew this would be the song for their first dance," I murmured to Chase.

He smiled as well. "It makes sense," he agreed. "Are you going to dance with me after this song?"

"Of course I'm going to. You can't go to a wedding and not dance."

When the song ended, everyone applauded and then other couples drifted onto the dance floor. Chase and I did the same and we danced to a couple of songs before I needed to take a break because of my leg. We sat back down at the table, and a moment later, Blake and Hailey joined us. Hailey waved her hand in front of her face. "Whew, it's hot in here."

Blake smiled. "That's because you haven't stopped moving since the reception began."

"Well, I'm not moving now, so hopefully I can cool off. Are you guys having fun?" she asked us.

"Yeah, it's a beautiful wedding," I told her. "I loved the song choice for your first dance."

She grinned. "We couldn't not use it," she admitted. "It's kind of our song."

Blake leaned in to kiss her cheek. "It was a good choice. But that's because it's one of the few things I actually had a say in."

We all laughed and chatted for a few more minutes. "So how is your adorable little nephew?" Hailey asked.

I dug my phone out and brought up a picture of him so I could show her. "He's getting bigger every day. I can't wait until he's old enough to come for a sleepover at our place."

"His mom is okay with you doing that?" she asked in surprise.

"Yeah. She's pretty much treating us like she would if Luke were still alive. We get to see Matthew whenever we want and when he's about a year old, we get to start having him for weekends and stuff. Cara is a really nice person."

"I can't wait until we have kids," Hailey said wistfully.

Blake had just taken a drink of water, and now he almost choked on it. Hailey helpfully patted him on the back, and he finally got his breath back. "Jesus Hailey. Are you trying to kill me?"

"Oh relax. I'm not saying we'll have them anytime soon," she said, rolling her eyes. "I'm just saying it'll be nice when we do have them."

Blake was noticeably paler now. "Right. Nice." He abruptly changed the subject. "You both start college in a few weeks, don't you?"

"Yeah, we're moving into our apartment in two weeks. It'll be weird not living on the farm," I said.

"At least you're going to college together," Hailey pointed out.

"That's true. And we'll be moving back to the farm after we've graduated. My parents are already talking about all the traveling they're planning on doing once we're back." I shook my head. "The only traveling those two have ever done is for horse shows. I'm not sure the world is ready for them to be tourists."

I heard the telltale rumble of a truck and trailer pull onto the parking lot. "Speaking of my parents, I think they've arrived. We're going to go give them a hand." Chase and I excused ourselves and left the tent to find my parents. They were just starting to unload Autumn, so we quickly moved in to give them a hand.

Twenty minutes later, he was hooked up and ready to go. Chase and I climbed onto the driver's bench while my parents went to let Hailey know we were ready. I clucked to Autumn and steered him to the entrance of the tent. A moment later, Blake and Hailey came out amongst many cheers and climbed into the back of the open carriage. I encouraged Autumn to move forward once more, and I maneuvered him out of the parking lot and onto the street.

The advantage to Hailey having one of the richest people in the world as her uncle was that he could make pretty much anything happen. The park the wedding had been held in was not usually used for weddings, but he'd pulled it off. The park was in the middle of the city, and he'd also managed to get the local police force to block off all the roads between the park and the hotel where Blake and Hailey were staying for the night. Apparently the hotel had special meaning to them, which is why they were spending the night there before going on their honeymoon.

I drove Autumn through the deserted streets, his hooves making a rhythmic sound against the pavement. We dropped

Hailey and Blake off at the front doors of the hotel, then turned around and headed back. I passed the reins over to Chase for the trip back, and he held them in one hand so he could wrap his other arm around me. I put my head on his shoulder and breathed out a sigh of contentment. We didn't speak on the way back, but we didn't need to. We both knew what the other was thinking, and for us, our love was often silent.

# Epilogue

I sat in my corner of the classroom, watching as students trickled in. My attention was caught by a girl who was on crutches, since I hadn't seen her before. She had long dark brown hair, but I couldn't see her eyes as she went to the seat in the other back corner of the room. She sat down and leaned back, closing her eyes and shoving her hands into the pocket of the hoodie that was too big for her.

I was curious in spite of myself. Who was this girl? Where had she been for the first and a half of classes? Why was she on crutches? She didn't have a cast on either leg, so I knew she didn't have a broken bone. I turned my attention away from her as more people came in, but I kept her in my periphery vision. I saw as a girl that obviously knew her sat beside her, but they didn't speak. And I saw when she recognized a guy at the front of the room. A slightly haunted expression flickered over her face before she turned away from him. I felt her eyes land on me, but I didn't turn to look at her.

The teacher came in and the class came to attention. I'd quickly decided that Mr. Ross wasn't a total douche, and I liked him as much as I ever liked any teacher. My opinion was solidified when he didn't say anything more than "Welcome back", to the new girl. Obviously, she wasn't actually new. My curiosity intensified, and for once I wished I actually talked to someone at the school so I could learn about her.

Mr. Ross told us to work on our projects, and then he surprised me by pairing me with the new girl, whose name I learned was Dana. I got out of my chair and moved over to her, sitting in the seat her friend had vacated. I looked over and met her eyes for the first time. They were hazel and would have been very pretty if it wasn't for the blank expression in them. But as I watched, they changed slightly and I saw intense pain enter them followed quickly by recognition. I knew it was because she saw the same thing in me, and something inside me loosened at the thought. Here was someone who had suffered as well, maybe more than I had.

Without a word, I took some papers out of my bag and handed them to her. She took them and started reading them while I sat back and did pretty much nothing for the rest of the class. When the bell rang, she handed the papers back to me and struggled to her feet. I had to stop myself from reaching out and helping her, which shocked me. Touching of any sort was abhorrent to me, so me wanting to help her was definitely unusual.

I waited until she was safely out of the way before I stood up and slung my bag over my shoulder. She left the classroom and stopped by her friend who was waiting just outside the door. I saw the guy she had recognized earlier go up behind her and place a hand on her shoulder. Part of me wanted to go and rip his hand off of her, but before I could move, she had shrugged the hand off and started moving away.

"Dana, wait. Please talk to me," the guy pleaded.

She shook her head. "I can't," she whispered, and then left as quickly as she could.

I saw the guy start to go after her, but Dana's friend stopped him with a hand on his arm. "Adam, don't. She needs more time before she talks to you."

"It's been six months, Cindy. I don't understand why she won't talk to me."

"I know she has her reasons, though I don't know what they are. But if you push her, she'll only pull away more."

"I never should have let her convince me to stop visiting her at the hospital," Adam said dejectedly.

"It wouldn't have mattered," Cindy replied. "She hasn't changed since she got out."

I walked by them then, so I didn't hear anything else. I went to my next class, but I barely paid attention as I thought about what could have happened to Dana. I knew it was something serious and that she'd been in the hospital for a little while at least, but I didn't know anything else.

The rest of the day passed without incident, and I was pleasantly surprised to find that Dana was in my last class as well. I sat next to her and she looked up when I set my binder on the desk. When I didn't say anything, she shrugged and we spent the class silently once again.

This time when the bell rang, I grabbed her bag before she could. I waited until she got to her feet and had her crutches in order, and then I handed the bag to her and walked away, a little embarrassed that I'd given in to my desire to help her.

I got into my car and drove home, arriving before either Bev or Carson were home. I went directly to my room and worked on my homework until Bev called me out for dinner. She asked how my day was and wasn't bothered when my only answer was to shrug. Carson got home just as she was setting dinner on the table, and we ate together in relative peace.

I did the dishes after dinner like I always did, then went to change into my jogging pants and hoodie. I tugged my shoes on at the front door and walked out. I started at a steady jog, but once I reached the park, I increased my speed. Trees flew by in a blur as my feet pounded into the ground. My breathing sped up and I revelled in the feel of my body responding when I poured on the speed.

I reached the other side of the park and slowed to a jog once again, heading back home. I walked back into the house and right to the shower, where I rinsed all the sweat off of me. I changed into a pair of pyjama bottoms and a fresh t-shirt, pulling it on quickly so I could avoid looking at the scars that covered the left side of my chest. I wandered out to the living room, where Bev was sitting and reading a book. I knew Carson was downstairs, but I didn't feel like watching TV with him right now. Instead, I grabbed a book for myself and sat on the chair opposite of where Bev was sitting. She offered me a brief smile before returning to her book.

When I grew tired, I stood up and put my book back. I hesitated in the doorway for a moment. "Good night," I mumbled.

Bev glanced up and smiled once more. "Good night Chase. See you in the morning."

I nodded and went to my room. I climbed into bed and as I drifted off to sleep, an image of Dana floated into my mind. I decided that maybe having one friend wouldn't be so horrible, and I fell asleep with that thought running through my mind.